To WB & EP

The best schools in the world

A novel by C.A.H. Arthur

Another inspired initiative

1

It was 7.30am at the Ministry for British Schools and there was already an excitable energy in the room. Although they were sitting around a large boardroom table, the room was a scene of individual industry, as members of the award-winning team taking schooling policy by storm poured over what the latest data was telling them. Spads Grant trembled as he emailed the group what he could have told them across the table. It took a few seconds for the chorus of gadgets to die down, as junior advisers clicked to read the latest reboot of the national schooling conversation.

"Our new schooling policies are guaranteed to transform this country's schools beyond recognition. But why should we stop there? Should we limit our aspirations for British schooling? Of course we shouldn't. We're going to unleash our can-do problem-solving to sort out school discipline once and for all. We're going to make the radical changes no one has ever dreamed of making before. We're going to outsource secondary school discipline into the criminal justice system."

The latest schooling hack dovetailed into Spads Grant's epic ambitions for British schooling. The Ministry for British Schools had been completely overhauled since the last general election. The re-election of the government underpinned this change, promising the usual reboot of British schooling. Eighteen months earlier, Grant had had the good fortune not to be on a duvet day when the cool new Prime Minister's latest publicity stunt touched down at his school. The visit was to showcase the repurposing of public buildings and wasn't strictly about schooling at all, but that didn't stop Grant elbowing his way into the limelight.

Prime Minister Front had come to power through his party's customary procedure, which resembled a palace coup. The love bombing and tactical schmoozing had served their purpose and were long gone. Now at the top of the pile, Front preferred planned interventions, freshly laundered through choice focus groups, on which he only had to dollop a generous serving of his own lyrical panache to get onto tomorrow's front pages. But when asked an unplanned question about how the children at

Grant's school would feel about being decanted onto the eleventh floor of a former call centre two miles away, Front wished he was sitting at the back.

But then he had a stroke of luck. Grant stood up and held the room for ten minutes with a case study about how he had prepared his own class to benefit from the change, set up as a cross curricular project. It didn't matter that the case study was fiction. Front realised instantly that Grant had the front to fabricate literally on this feet. He needed more of this sort who could embellish any story to suit the moment and fit in perfectly with the substance-light sound bites his government excelled at. This man needed a role in schooling policy, an area that had worked for Front in the past, but now plagued him.

Grant's school didn't need much persuading to release him with immediate effect. Front threw resources at him, resulting in the formation of a team committed to policy flipping paradigm shifts, prepared to make things up inside any government ministry for the good of the boss. Front finally had enough pawns in place to play his hand as the leader of the age. He called a snap general election, won a landslide victory and the rest, he thought, was history.

2

Spads Grant proudly surveyed his team, always eager to respond to his ever-changing priorities, grateful as they were to be elevated up to the dizzying heights of radical policy experimentation. There had been a step change in the frequency of initiatives seeping out of the Ministry for British Schools since the last election, with Spads as the self-styled lead senior adviser for schooling hacks, ready to act out his brainwaves on the widest possible stage. Spads was the ultimate glass half full, eager to learn the secrets of packaging and even managing continuous change. To the Prime Minister, this seemed to fit in perfectly with the interplay of media and electoral cycles, and secured his access to No.10 for now.

Spads sold his inconsistencies as a game changer. He was always happy to change his mind to follow the latest evidence, and made no apologies for dropping initiatives that weren't working. He wasn't afraid of U-turns. In fact, U-turns kept the

Ministry for British Schools trending, proving it always made sense to value messaging above everything else.

Families could sleep more easily knowing the latest stewards of British schooling policy integrated all prior failures into their latest hand break turn for the good of all children. When they started to have successes, these would be integrated too.

3

Spads' first significant achievement in government was his handling of the fallout from the first major schooling initiative he oversaw. A ground-breaking concept in modern times, the headline-grabbing version of back to basics preschooling had been conceived by his deputy, Cosmina Blame. She joined the schooling policy circus the weekend after Front's landslide election victory.

Grant to Blame … Friday … 23:57

The PM's an electoral genius. He's creating a live manifesto to be ready for another snap general election. Need to polish off schooling hacks to pitch to No. 10 on Monday.

What do you think of this?

This government's mission is to have the best schools in the world. We will help every child achieve our new national standard for British schooling. And if anyone does manage to fall behind, we will instruct them to be helped.

All of this will be achieved during the school day. No need for homework, parents' evenings or even school reports when it's impossible for children not to succeed. No need for exams that stress out families at home when children will graduate from the best schools in the world with all the knowledge they really need. Guaranteed.

And because children will have their lives set up by the age of eighteen, university can concentrate on the social side of things older children really care about. This government is determined to sort British schooling out once and for all.

Blame to Grant ... Saturday ... 00:01

What an amazing ambition for British schooling. You mention knowledge. What about skills?

Grant to Blame ... Saturday ... 00:05

I've cracked the new curriculum for British schooling consumers. Reading and copying out for every lesson from early years to sixth form. No need for exams and fool-proof teacher assessment – the teacher simply signs off the lesson when the child has copied out the text. Take maths. Every child will meet the standard of the model answers!

Every child will graduate from school with their own copied out volumes of the cracking new curriculum to take home as a reference library. And this is the really clever bit. We're building a knowledge-based economy fit for the information age, so no skills are needed.

Blame to Grant ... Saturday ... 00:07

I've never seen schooling taken to places like this before.

Fool-proof assessment means teacher training can be completed in no time at all. Why not centralise teacher training within the Ministry for British Schools itself?

Grant to Blame ... Saturday ... 00:09

You're right! I can see you've got a can-do attitude towards schooling too.

If we get the national standard right every child will achieve it and we'll keep parents happy. With all lessons based on copying out from a textbook we can train teachers in weeks and save money to focus on more interesting schooling hacks.

Blame to Grant ... Saturday ... 00:13

I see even bigger benefits. Why not take the opportunity to put learning back in its proper place?

Grant to Blame ... Saturday ... 00:13

Interesting. Give me a narrative I can integrate into my pitch.

Blame to Grant ... Saturday ... 00:15

Here you go.

Can we afford to keep kicking the schooling can down the road? Shouldn't your child's schooling fully prepare them for their future? We are the government with the ambition to create the best schools in the world, schooling that means no one has to waste the rest of their life learning.

Grant to Blame ... Saturday ... 00:16

Looks like we're on the same wavelength.

I need someone like you to work with me at the Ministry. When could you start?

Blame to Grant ... Saturday ... 00:16

Monday morning. I'll e mail my agency now.

4

The first thing that must be said about Cosmina Blame is that Spads Grant considered her to be the deputy lead senior adviser for schooling hacks in the government. Not the lead senior adviser – that was him. But she was the deputy lead senior adviser, freed from the constraints of decades of schooling research, allowing her to respond like a superconductor to what the latest data about schooling was telling her. She was proud of being fickle about the school experiences of children in times defined by constant change. Children knew this better than adults, which she understood as the proud mother of three virtual children inside an online simulation.

And she had an efficiency that put others to shame. One Sunday afternoon she introduced Victorian elementary school discipline to her virtual family – Exam, aged 15, Project, aged 11, and Play, aged 3. When she pressed return their schooling outcome scores increased by 11, 24 and 50 per cent. Cosmina congratulated herself on her brainwave. No physical contact was possible inside a computer simulation, or needed in real life. Shouting at children to work and play more productively was enough.

The lead senior adviser for schooling hacks was speechless when the deputy lead adviser shared her discovery and within six months a chain of no-nonsense preschools, sponsored by a martial arts and soft furnishings franchise, was being rolled out across the country to support young children into the saddle of schooling through a historically-inspired approach to school discipline.

5

The national launch of the draconian preschools was an eventful week. On the Monday Prime Minister Front opened one of the revolutionary new preschools in his own Domesboroughton constituency. Grant and Blame were also in attendance to oversee media-friendly parents despatching their young children down a long winding path, and through a gate that hid the actual entrance with its harsh chant of school rules by a virtual Victorian factory overseer.

By Tuesday the complaints started coming into the artificial intelligence headteacher who oversaw the whole thing, a Spads Grant cost saving idea that proved a shrewd move, as human headteachers would have needed police protection from the vitriol of the complaints.

The headteacher interface also created capacity for an attempt to save the new initiative, but a bit less shouting and lower fines for talking couldn't prevent it being abandoned by the Thursday. Front led the announcement himself, linked to a cabinet reshuffle in which he held the existing Secretary of State for British Schools fully accountable for the latest schooling crisis.

The Prime Minister had sacrificed another Cabinet minister to cling on at the top. This was the day when Valentine Vaklerner was removed from one of the great Ministries of State and sent to the Ministry for British Schools to sort out the mess.

"You there, Vaklerner? We've got a crisis on our hands."

"Another crisis, Prime Minister? Not "it's the Home Office because it's happening in this country" again, is it? Who's messed up this time?"

"It's Schools again. We need know-it-all Vaklerner to put out the fire. I've tried to support him, but he's got to go. Had to clear out his minister too. Listen, we've got groups of parents refusing to buy into the vision."

"Who on earth thought making children cry was acceptable?"

"Listen! We're getting hundreds of complaints by the hour, mostly against me! Why me, I ask you?"

"Just a thought, Prime Minister. Perhaps because you appropriated another inspired initiative as your own idea?"

Valentine's sarcasm only elicited a growl, so he carried on.

"At least you've got a narrative for clearing out those fools who've been making the wrong sort of headlines about schooling. Although I can't see why the Home Office should be involved this time."

"Shut up and listen, Vaklerner. Grant's ideas really get people talking."

"Indeed they do, so wh..."

"So I'm keeping him at Schools. That's why I'm sending you there to draw a line under this week. Grant cooks up the kind of radical hacks we need to keep voters interested."

"Even after this week's mess, Prime Minister? Are you being serious?"

"LISTEN. Grant's rough edges could be a real asset for this government. If he can come up with something that actually works, we've got plenty of comms to sort out the messaging."

"So I'm expected to accept a demotion, am I, to a ministry with crisis baked into the walls?"

"Don't dis schooling: it's this government's top priority. Late for a meeting. I need your answer now."

"I shouldn't be put in this position, Prime Minister. Why shouldn't I just resign?"

"Accept or resign, but I need your answer NOW!"

"So you beat me to the party leadership, and now you're giving me no choice."

"Thank you, but I must say I'm very disappointed. Need to ring my second choice now."

"Stop playing games, Prime Minister! I'm not leaving the Home Office."

"Yes you are, know-it-all. Lazy Strong deserves a trial at the Home Office. Everyone knows she's the hardest working member of the Cabinet. And who knows, I might even drop the lazy one day."

"Like you did with know-it-all?"

"I accept your resignation."

"I'm not resigning. Who am I getting as my deputy?"

"No need for any more schooling ministers of state with special advisers like Grant and his team. You'll be called the Minister for British Schools so the public don't get confused. Get there no later than seven tomorrow morning. You'll soon see how Grant gives value for money."

At this Front ended the call leaving Valentine Vaklerner's head racing. He clutched at a mental balance sheet to make sense of his abrupt change of circumstances. On the debit side Front's clear intention was to stage-manage his political demise. His desk at the Home Office was already being cleared, and his driver tomorrow morning would take him to his new office at a government ministry close to failing its stress tests. On the credit side, it was always reassuring to experience Front's imposter syndrome first hand. Front quickly abandoned the superficial charm with him for a tightrope of assertion and aggression. It suggested the PM wasn't yet in an unassailable position.

While being driven to his first day in his new job, Valentine tried to be open-minded about his new special adviser. Was Grant an unclassifiable political genius capable of turning British schooling around? Was the abolition of public exams a strategic hack to pave the way for revolutionary change? Or was Grant in thrall to his own narratives in the world of endless possibilities the Prime Minister had granted him? Were Grant and his team going to take the nation's schooling over a cliff?

Valentine was resigned to finding out the hard way.

6

One thing Valentine did know: he wasn't going to give up without a fight. The scale of his task became clear on arrival at his new ministry. He'd expected formal introductions, but he was a sideshow to a role play taking place in the collaboration amphitheatre outside his new office. Blame was playing a parent complaining about one of the draconian preschools, with Grant standing in to demonstrate the new frontier in school leadership being forged by machine learning. The audience of junior schooling advisers was spellbound.

"Hey, dye wanna punish that teacher who told off your kid?"

"Can I be the one doing the punishing?"

"Don't worry about that. We do it for ye. That's what us school leaders are for. Or dye wanna trade in punishment for cool family rewards?"

"What punishments can I choose from?"

"It's boring, but we call 'em sanctions. End your complaint within an hour to qualify. See there on the screen? Click on the troll in the school reception and you could give the teacher extra marking, an impossible deadline, longer working days or even shorter school holidays!"

"Amazing. Can I cut their summer holidays? I'd really like that."

"Yeah, thanks to our new flexible teacher contracts! We could extend working hours at short notice, although we would need to give the teacher twelve hours' notice. But if you're lucky, they could be abroad and need to book a return flight."

"Amazing! This government is finally listening to parents. What are the cool rewards you mentioned?"

"Click there. See? You've been allocated a three minute phone call with the teacher responsible."

"I don't understand."

See how the countdown's changed? Trade in your sanction within the next fifteen minutes and get entered into the new schooling lottery draw on Christmas Eve. Win your kid a place in their first choice of preschool. Any preschool, anywhere: starting in January!"

"How can a phone call be a sanction?"

"It can if you give them a hard time."

"Only fifteen minutes to decide?"

"Yeah, but think about parents not lucky enough to have something to complain about."

"But won't a lottery disappoint thousands of kids pinning their careers on getting a new preschool place for Christmas? How many lottery winners will there be?"

"No one's going to be disappointed. Just being entered in the new lottery will fire up kids' career ambitions at the very start of their schooling lives. Can't give details yet, but the Ministry are negotiating for private preschools to be included. They'll announce the number of winners at the same time."

"But I'd feel cheated out of making that teacher pay. Is it worth it just to get a better schooling lottery ticket?"

"I'm glad you asked. This is the really clever bit. When you enter the new lottery your kid gets their own *I want better schooling* sweatshirt, allowed in line with new national school uniform policy to keep teachers on their toes. And you get your own car sticker and entry into the lottery social media group with shopping offers until the draw on Christmas Eve."

"Amazing! Now I understand. I'd always choose a better lifestyle before some petty vendetta. If anyone's gonna strut around that preschool it's gonna be my little kid!"

"Yeah, and you don't want other lucky lottery entrants looking down at you at the school gates, do you?"

"You're right. It's a no-brainer. Do I still have enough time to trade in my complaint and enter the government's new schooling lottery?"

"Yeah, click there. The troll hasn't eaten the reception desk yet."

7

Valentine thought it best to go with the flow at his new ministry for the time being. He allowed Grant and his team to take all the credit for using AI to close down the torrent of parental complaints against the failed preschools in only two weeks. He even allowed them to award themselves an award for political escapology, the highest level of praise in the government.

So the up-front government-backed schooling lottery was born, extended to primary schools and scheduled to be drawn on Christmas Eve by the Prime Minister himself, who appropriated the idea as his own. No.10 waited for clear signs the new lottery had captured the public mood before confirming there would be five annual winners, but that private preschools and prep schools were not going to be included. The government had prevented social unrest with an impressively meagre outlay.

Valentine's political antenna fully understood the desperate situation he was in, demoted and readied for political humiliation. He therefore judged it best to act as a new Minister for British Schools every bit as eccentric as his new ministry, and to sit behind this persona until the political landscape improved. The air of dilettante curiosity he now cultivated acted as a mask to shield lesser mortals from his anguish about the damage to national schooling being planned by a cabal of special advisers proud of rejecting decades of research. His auditory memory held, with real time recall, the data that could have expelled his special advisers out of the stage door. But he knew that breaking cover was not an option until events gave him a window of opportunity.

Because he wasn't there to do much beyond rubber stamp radical schooling hacks and carry the can for the fallout,

Valentine found he had more thinking time than he was used to as a senior minister. He used this to evaluate strategies for recovering the situation, and to think of affectations to alienate him from his civil servants and support the theatre of his good working relationships with Grant and his team.

He was helped in this by Front's decision to bring forward the promise of a complete schooling revolution into the current parliament, expanding Grant's workload exponentially, and resulting in him milking all his contacts for potential schooling hacks. Grant therefore took his one to one meetings with his minister seriously; in case they produced anything he could perform alchemy on to maintain his indispensability in the eyes of the PM. This allowed Valentine to feed information through Grant that helped him learn more about the contours of his new situation.

8

Valentine's first success with his new persona was his suggestion that science should be removed from the revolutionary new schooling curriculum and replaced by a new, indispensable on-trend subject; shopping know-how. He tried this out first on his civil servants with a delivery so dry they believed him. Valentine derived two distinct pleasures from this. He liked the impression they thought their boss was a fool who needed to be humoured out of the door. But he relished how well they thought they were shielding their disdain from him: they weren't.

Valentine gained useful insights from the sequence of events triggered when he championed shopping know-how as a curriculum staple with Grant. It was on course to be a typical Monday meeting to chart the week ahead.

"...and, luckily, I know who can get the history and technology sections of the cracking new schooling curriculum back on track for the live launch on Christmas Eve. By the way, the junior advisers think they've found the perfect armchair for the PM's curriculum story time. It's going to be spellbinding!"

"I agree, Spads; the launch is going to be unforgettable. Let's put the armchair on our agenda for next week. We need a plan to repair the biggest cracks in the new schooling curriculum. Who do you propose? Not the same person, I presume?"

"Of course not. One's a neighbour of mine. She's a teacher who's taken a gap year to become a proper historian."

"Is she a history teacher?"

"She's written histories of Athens and Rome this week, so I know she can catch up the time wasted by all those disagreements in the history committee."

"It's a shame the historians effectively sacked themselves. What books has she written?"

"No books yet, more articles."

"OK. What history journals and magazines should I look up?"

"Not history publications specifically, she's working on widening the appeal of serious history. Look up *vac hacks*. Now click on *Rome in an afternoon*."

"So, she's a travel writer? Oh, I see: more a travel blogger. What qualifies her to write a cracking new history section for the cracking new curriculum?"

"See for yourself. Read how she's summed up Roman history in five hundred words, and I'm told Rome has quite a lot of history."

"Get her to submit an online application today. Now, technology, not another neighbour?"

"No, and no need to interview. I gave the old technology curriculum to our current employee of the month. He asks no questions at all and delivers 100% on time. Everything's "no probs" with him."

Spads theatrically traced quotation marks in the air.

"He's already rattled off half of primary technology in a week, and he's overcome that annoying old habit of having practical technology lessons. We're thinking of making him into an acting senior junior schooling adviser."

"We'll interview for history on Thursday and go with "no probs" for now.

Valentine even more theatrically traced quotation marks in the air. Spads looked impressed.

"Make sure you book in a week of quality assurance for both subjects with civil servants by the end of next month."

"Thank you, minister. I'll get Cosmina straight onto it after we finish."

"One more thing, Spads. The science curriculum is still looking far too long. I think I may have found a solution that could trend around the world ... if we dare do it."

Valentine paused for heightened theatrical effect.

"Take science completely out of the schooling curriculum, and replace it with another evidence-based subject... like shopping know-how."

Grant froze. He was rarely lost for words. He sat for nearly a minute thinking. Valentine's hunch he wouldn't differentiate between science and shopping might be right.

"How can we sell it to the public?"

Valentine made his move.

"We can explain that science is developing very quickly these days, so it's better to take science completely out of the curriculum because we won't tolerate years of out of date copying out. We can promise to keep the situation under review and reinstate science if things settle down. We can then cast shopping know-how as part of the retail renaissance we're committed to."

"Don't consumer tastes change too?"

"They do, but most fashions are cyclical, so nothing remains out of date for too long. We can make a seismic impact on schooling with this single hack."

"I like it! We could hand over the shopping know-how curriculum to a group of social media influencers and serialise extracts in the press before the PM's Christmas launch."

"Won't that mean more bun fights about content, Spads?"

"I hear what you're saying, minister, but spats between influencers will trend better."

"Sorry, Spads. You're right. We can make history: the first country that dares end school science experiments and has children planning shopping sprees instead."

"I can see us top trending with this, minister! Can I get Cosmina on board?"

"Of course, Spads. Who better to make the most from this opportunity than the two most radical thinkers in Whitehall?"

9

Grant tripped on the carpet while launching from his chair in his eagerness to consult with his deputy. Valentine was lucky

Blame was conducting one of her answer and answer sessions in the collaboration amphitheatre at that moment, giving him a clear view of the excitement his idea generated. The gesticulating alternated between them until Blame ran to get a newspaper. Blame said something and they seemed to morph into one entity, heading towards his door. Valentine quickly knocked some papers onto the floor so he wouldn't be seen observing them as they entered. There was no knocking on the door or standing on ceremony.

"Cosmina's cracked it! She's knows an associate editor at a national newspaper who'll jump at the chance to serialise extracts from the new shopping know-how curriculum ahead of the Christmas launch."

"Her paper's always looking out for new lifestyle hacks."

"And we can sell compulsory school shopping know-how as the must-have new thing!" Spads seemed about to levitate.

Valentine took the excitement in their eyes as a chance to push things a little further.

"Thank you, Cosmina. No one values modern consumerism quite like you. Can I discuss a few details with Spads, and then you can take it from there?"

Blame turned around at the door to relish her starring role in the schooling soap opera.

"You see, minister, the secret is to overestimate and overvalue, so you always get more than you expect."

Now alone with Grant, Valentine upped the ante.

"Happy for you to take this to No.10 as your own idea, Spads. But do make sure you get clearance to oversee schooling innovations like this. I shouldn't really be telling you this, but the Prime Minister often dabbles in something new he thinks has traction, and then takes credit for the whole thing. Look at how he's already passed off the new schooling lottery as his own idea. Just be careful, Spads. The PM's greedy for any policy limelight, whatever the cost to our careers."

Grant's expression tightened; taken aback by the first direct criticism of the Prime Minister he had ever heard Valentine utter. But Valentine had sensibly dangled the policy goodies first, on which Grant easily fixated.

"I'll sell it as an unmissable schooling brainwave and show him how, in our safe hands, we'll make headlines around the world!"

The gambit seemed to be on. Grant had taken the bait. But the real prize was giving Grant an insight into the Prime Minister's dabbling. Valentine knew in his bones that Front and Grant's overweening egos could only collaborate so far.

10

Valentine's wait to discover the Prime Minister's take on shopping know-how in the core curriculum felt like an age. He agreed to appoint Spads' friend to write the history section of the cracking new curriculum, even though she answered his question about the Cold War implying Afghanistan had a coastline on the Black Sea. He even allowed Cosmina to get away with removing a civil servant from the Ministry.

It happened on the Friday with Spads out of the office, probably having his meeting with the PM. When Spads' deputy acted up in his absence her zeal had nothing to restrain it. Cosmina often gathered the awestruck junior schooling hackers in the collaboration amphitheatre for a motivational monologue. She didn't expect questions about her vision, and certainly didn't expect suggestions for improvement. So when a junior civil servant, no less, pitched in with a helpful suggestion, Cosmina saw red.

"Because we're writing a definitive curriculum, shouldn't we allow teachers more judgement with assessment? Shouldn't we let children take short breaks from copying out the curriculum to tell their teachers what they understand?"

The poor civil servant was only trying to help, but she'd broken a cardinal rule. Senior special advisers at the Ministry for British Schools should not be given advice. Within the hour she was being walked out of the office by Cosmina. Although, judging by their pleasant conversation, she'd probably been instructed to welcome being held accountable for her mistake.

"I don't think you'll be needing this," Cosmina broadcast across the open office, reaching into the lift to remove the Ministry for British Schools thermal mug ostentatiously from the civil servant's personal effects.

"Remember," Cosmina shouted once the lift doors had closed, "we don't put pressure like that on teachers, especially the ones trained here at the Ministry. They get confused very easily."

The general dysfunction within his new ministry helped Valentine let this pass as a minor episode. The ministry's civil servants kept a low profile, busying themselves with the most routine work they could justify, trying to hang onto their careers.

It turned out the civil servant despatched by Cosmina was grateful for her redeployment to another ministry, and most of her former colleagues were more envious than anything else. Valentine informed Spads about the redeployment at their next Monday one to one after a long item about the PM's armchair for the Christmas launch. Spads pretended to be interested.

"What did the Prime Minister say about changing curriculum subjects?" Valentine tried to put on an air of detached curiosity.

"He liked it in principle, thought it could grab headlines at the next summit, but he didn't like the exit strategy. Said he couldn't carry off a successful U-turn simply by reinstating science in the schooling curriculum. Apparently, with science, gaps in knowledge matter."

"What do you mean, Spads? Didn't you work up a convincing U-turn before you presented the idea to the Prime Minister? I thought you understood the way he likes to do things? Does he have a downer on us now?"

"No, he likes the new curriculum, thinks it can give the party a wider appeal. He even suggested I didn't need to hurry to get the team in place to write version 2. Gives me time to work on something much more interesting than the schooling curriculum. I'm thinking something about behaviour."

Reading the runes, Valentine sensed that Spads had probably passed off shopping know-how as his minister's idea, but that sent the Prime Minister a message: he was surfing his new predicament nicely. He felt a pang of pity for Spads, who clearly didn't realise delaying version 2 of the curriculum, was a code he couldn't read about his own Whitehall shelf life. He had to give Front credit for mixing up a heady cocktail of admonition, praise and hope to keep Spads uncertain and pliable. But Front probably wouldn't suspect the real gift Spads had received from his minister, the knowledge that the PM would try to permanently exclude him from his own schooling revolution one day. What sort of a fight would Spads put up to avoid that fate?

The end of today's meeting left Valentine feeling he was beginning to get a handle on his new situation, and he could now see the next few steps ahead. His suspicion remained intact that Front would use Spads Grant to bring him down at the allotted time. But he could make use of Spads' uncertainty and the surprising respect he showed his minister, despite having the PM's ear. Above all, he resolved to continue crafting his new profile as an eccentric but open-minded Minister for British Schools, feeding his special advisers minor morsels to see whether they had any ability at all to shape a promising idea into a policy proposal.

Valentine Vaklerner sensed he was in a secure-ish position for now. He steeled himself for the visual, auditory and kinaesthetic learning journey ahead of him, embedded as he was at the centre of a revolution in British schooling from which no one in the country was safe.

Trust me

1

The Prime Minister's first name was Pleasant, passed down his mother's line and forced into an uneasy alliance with his father's family, the Drivellings. Pleasant and his mother had been managing each other for as long as he could remember. She was like an engine driving him on, always revving in the background whether he liked it or not. She held the purse strings tightly, so he played along. She forced him to endure her nickname for him through school and university. She told him "Dependable" was character building, even more so in his case because his drivelling could always be depended on.

Dependable's defining moment at boarding school came at a hustings for the youth parliament. In his re-election pitch, he promised to improve the school bank's credit rating. But when someone shouted, "he broke the bank himself," the room erupted in a chorus of dissent. "Too many vanity projects", "who needs an armchair in a school gym?"; "don't depend on Dependable's drivelling." So ended Dependable's first punt at a career in politics. He still felt good about himself, though. None of the other candidates got a reaction to match his.

In his final year at university, he earned a rare maternal compliment when he blackmailed her to revert to his real name to kick-start the political career he was set on. This got his foot in a few think tank doors while he bided his time waiting for the nod back in Domesboroughton.

It was no coincidence that Domesboroughton was his mother's family seat, which she ruled from their ancient pile resembling a dungeon above ground on a hill. She viewed her patch like a rotten borough and dominated the party's constituency association accordingly, scanning the rank and file at meetings to keep them in line. The ranks themselves knew it was best to keep to the tightly-scripted agendas she provided, because drawing attention to yourself risked being hit by a command you knew you would follow without question. They all remembered the meeting where she resurrected an old Georgian use of the term shopping to rubber stamp her son as the candidate for one the safest of Parliamentary seats. Two members later resigned to get answers about why they had followed her order to sit on top of the man who had voted against Pleasant in the cancelled first ballot. He stayed on to become a Drivelling loyalist, clearly seeing the error of his ways.

2

When he entered the Commons a few days before his twenty-ninth birthday, the new Member of Parliament for Domesboroughton basked in an inner glow cast by the real start of his political career. He was grateful for the timing of the general election, allowing him to meet his mother's target for getting elected. In his maiden speech he styled himself as Pleasant Drivelling, a political superhero in waiting. This had been a planned move for years, to lever him into the Cabinet where his cult of personality could emerge. He was helped by having his mother as his constituency secretary. She was outstanding in the role, nipping onerous commitments in the bud and allowing him to concentrate on the Westminster intrigues that mattered. After only four months as a backbencher, Pleasant was approached by a junior minister and began to edge ahead of his intake.

"Pleasant Drivelling, isn't it? Hepton Royd. I've just been appointed as the minister responsible for policy flip-flopping at the Ministry of Political know-how. Is it right you cut your teeth in one of those citizen focus groups?"

"That's right. My first paid job after university, but I left to set up my own think tank."

"I didn't know that?"

"Yes, we did one of those important pieces of work that should sit on every political think tank's shelves these days."

"Why haven't I heard about this? What did you do?"

"We tried to get first time voters interested in politics by following them on holiday, and showing them how to build a fully-functioning political polis while chilling on the beach."

"No. I still can't place it. Why is it essential reading?"

"Because we showed it doesn't really work. At best they set up their own beach city state and voted to ostracise us to get on with their holiday. At worst we needed police protection. We were hiring in our own private security at the end."

"Sounds like you already understand the burdens we have to suffer for this political life."

"Oh, I do. It was hard work flying around the world for two years, the Med for half the year, East Asia and Australia in the winter. It really wasn't easy setting up in a new villa every couple of weeks, to turn up unannounced and get the uncorrupted data we needed. Anyway, why the interest in citizen focus groups?"

"Here's the thing. One of them's made a radical turn. They've become a superconductor to manage policy flip-flopping, providing the messaging a government needs to get itself out of a tight spot."

Pleasant's political antenna twitched. "Sorry, I don't understand. What do you mean?"

"The master stroke is stoking peer group competition from a lifestyle angle. They've built up a monster focus group of citizens from marginal seats who buy into must-have new thing consumerism as the best way to get to their best lives. They compete to stay in the group with the justifications a government needs for any policy or policy U-turn."

"Are you saying that...?"

"Yes, the new policies come from us, but they give us the messaging for the policy and the U-turn if the policy flops. We launch a new policy with an initial sound bite well short of a cliché, so people don't get too attached to it. If the policy fails, or something better turns up, we've already got the messaging to pivot into the exit strategy. Planned policy flip-flopping is promising an electoral jackpot: U-turns baked into the cake that can even increase support for the government!"

"You've really got my attention now, Hepton. How can U-turns make a government more popular?"

"This is the unbelievable bit. The focus group has helped us understand how we can regain control of a failing policy area by levelling up with the electorate that life's a lottery. We can earn kudos for being honest, and save money by promoting health, housing, schooling etc. as lotteries, and using examples of voters who win as policy successes."

Pleasant wanted a piece of this pie, so suppressed his enthusiasm. "Sounds quite interesting, Hepton."

"Glad to hear that, Pleasant, because I want you to become my Parliamentary Private Secretary. A colleague from Domesboroughton recommended you."

Pleasant added a hint of coy to maintain his cover.

"If I can see the focus group in action, I can let you know."

3

Pleasant Drivelling conducted the next meeting of the citizen consumers like a celebrity topping the bill. He ignored his observer status immediately, steering a discussion about property-owning democracy into a competition to find the most outrageous examples of rivalry and benchmarking between neighbours. With the group in a frenzy over home improvements, he introduced a new angle they could all agree on: planning rules were far too restrictive. Then, with the help of a very vocal member of the group, Pleasant conjured some policy messaging out of the ether.

Say goodbye to the bad old days of planning with *do owt t' yer 'ouse.* No need for planning permission at all when you could apply a simple process to give yourself permission to do anything you wanted to improve your home, your biggest single stake as a citizen consumer. They all felt positive about being able to oversee a much quicker process themselves, posting their self-reviewed plans on the internet for no obligation consultation. The value of their homes would boom, and so would the economy.

Pleasant waited a good minute for someone in the group to realise that limitless home improvements might create problems, but no one said anything. So he pitched in with scenarios to complete the exit strategy. If *do owt t' yer 'ouse* got out of control, if too many people ignored helpful feedback, the policy could be stopped, but it wouldn't be fair on people who hadn't taken advantage of the new system. So it might be better to get experts to re-evaluate everything, replacing *do owt t' yer 'ouse* with *do nowt t' yer 'ouse,* giving planning authorities the powers they needed to take back control.

Even though this was a focus group that aimed to please, Pleasant earned a standing ovation at the end of the session and agreed, yes, to be Hepton Royd's PPS with immediate effect.

Pleasant sensed a potential opportunity, if he played his cards right. Hepton could be career positive for him, at least for now.

4

Pleasant quite liked being a Parliamentary Private Secretary. His next real goal was to get into the Cabinet, which conferred the delegation of detail to Ministers of State. He didn't relish having to do a stint as a junior minister, encumbered by policy implementation and outcomes. He was content for now playing in the realm of pure ideas, which didn't feel like work at all.

But what did annoy Pleasant was sharing a tiny Westminster office with Hepton. He didn't like people getting an inside track on how he operated in real time. He started off by flooding Hepton with complements as a disarming tactic. This extended the honeymoon phase of their relationship, and helped Pleasant detect a route worth exploring to uncover weakness.

Although he boasted about faking it even after he made it, Hepton often took issues much more seriously than anyone would expect from an authentic careerist. Pleasant perceived his relative advantage – he could pick up and drop positions effortlessly to serve his self-interest. But he still had to tread carefully. Hepton had to be managed up as a mentor and remain blissfully unaware he was really a stepping stone for Pleasant to use at the right moment.

An office exchange between them laid the foundations for Pleasant's next important manoeuvre. They had been separately working the room in a Commons reception for public sector-facing software companies, trying out potential policy hacks. Hepton thought this worthwhile; a chance to get a feel for the policy proposals that information platforms could manage. Pleasant wasn't convinced: every executive he talked to was positive they could provide the software the government needed to manage and evaluate every policy punt he threw at them – dentist raffles, junk food passports, prison rail, pet pensions. Pleasant was having to put on a theatrical air with Hepton in the room. Then Pleasant had a stroke of luck. Hepton caught his eye, gesturing he had to leave, an emergency, and scurried off.

Pleasant relaxed and joined a ring of spectators locked on a waiter whose voice was dipped to a whisper. It turned out the waiter had an axe to grind, a grudge against his former boss, a software executive somewhere else in the room. The waiter claimed he was sacked because he told his boss what he'd pitched to the government was undeliverable. But there was a real prize for the politicians present: he named the Cabinet minister who fell for it, whose ministry was wasting shed-loads of public money on a flawed policy hack.

Hepton was staring gloomily into his computer when Pleasant burst into their office, barely able to contain his excitement at having top grade gossip to pass on.

"You missed the best bit by far."

"So, which ideas did your lot like? Any techy pitches set up yet?"

"Yeah, yeah, yeah, they all liked everything, but you'll want to hear this first. A group of us heard a waiter with a grudge letting rip. He'd been sacked as a software engineer by one of the companies in the room, but the good bit is he named the Cabinet minister who fell for a pitch he told his boss just can't work. That's why he was sacked. You missed a treat."

"Can we focus on the policy proposals, Pleasant?" Hepton wanted to get down to business, but Pleasant was still fixated on the waiter's revelations.

"Fess Uppleby has fallen for a policy hack he's going to regret. He's bought fortune telling software to set bespoke business rates for every business in the country."

"You're getting side-tracked, Pleasant. Can we stick to why we were there? We're both of us going nowhere if we don't get our ideas picked up."

"But I thought you'd want to know about Fess. Isn't he the pack leader from your intake?"

At this Hepton stopped talking and held Pleasant with a fixed stare. Pleasant stared back, slowly exchanging his grin for a safer blank look.

"We got the most offers for junk food passports in the healthy eating strategy. Should be able to confirm the IT pitches by the end of this week. Anything extra I can help with, Hepton, you looked hassled when you left?"

Hepton suddenly lightened up. "Thanks, Pleasant. Breakfast meetings best for me. I need to sort out the mess with the new community sports grants. Turns out a press release was issued this morning announcing, and I quote, *we can confirm that the first of the new community sports grants will go to areas.*"

"What areas?"

"Exactly. Someone's met a deadline without having anything to say!"

"Not unheard of."

"I know. I've got seventy-two hours to work up criteria to channel the money where we want it."

Perhaps Hepton was stressed. Perhaps he really wanted to know about Fess Uppleby. But Pleasant needed to guarantee his disarming worked, so he did something he normally avoided.

"Don't envy you that, Hepton, but if I can lighten the load in any way, the offer's there."

"Maybe. Perhaps you could conduct the next citizen focus group meeting for me. Things have got so bad at the Ministry for British Schools they've asked us to lift some of the load with some messaging to help them out. The brief is to make parents accept that higher schooling standards need harder exams with more children failing. It's on the same deadline as the sports grant criteria, so if you could clear a bit of space for me I'd be grateful."

"Consider it done."

"Thanks for this, Pleasant. There's a meeting of the focus group tomorrow, but a word of advice: don't think we can guarantee they'll give us the messaging we need. Yes they're competitive, but sometimes we have to abandon meetings if their egos get waxed too much and their sense of entitlement takes over. No pressure, but we need some messaging that can be used in days so Schools can claw back control of its agenda."

"Don't worry, Hepton. I'll get them to deliver a new line on exams with an exit strategy that meets your high standards."

"OK, Pleasant. It needs to work for both of us, or we might replace Fess in the team room gossip."

"Trust me, Hepton. You're in safe hands."

5

Pleasant Drivelling had unexpectedly landed himself in the middle of a key issue the government needed to resolve. The previous government had undermined itself with its obsession for targets and layers of pseudo-scientific measurement. When they committed to a sea change in schooling attainment in a single parliament, they had to find ways of making qualifications easier. Their master stroke was continuous assessment completed by children themselves. The government initially basked in schooling success, but when the consequences of children marking their own work played out in wider society, the Opposition's pledge to bring back better qualifications helped seal their decisive election defeat.

It was obvious that the new government came in with a ticket based on increasing schooling standards, but large swathes of parents weren't happy when their children failed the first set of new, more challenging exams. Parents had been promised a gradual increase in exam difficulty with teachers having more time to deliver the new, more challenging curriculum. But the government wanted a headline about schooling standards in its first year so increased grade boundaries radically, not realising this had echoes of the previous government's arbitrary shifts to schooling standards.

Pleasant was now responsible for the messaging to make very challenging exams attractive to voters. As always, he wore his responsibility lightly; a chance for playful experimentation. He met with the focus group the next day, but didn't get the welcome he'd expected. He put this down to the betas in the group being cleared out and replaced: they had given him his standing ovation last time. The alphas were still there, goading all comers to try and engage them. Also, his ruse about planning permission was hypothetical, and he was helped by being a cool new face at the time. Now the difficult ones were embedded and many of them had a direct stake as parents. Some had children who had sat the latest set of exams. One vented their frustration.

"If he'd left school last year he'd have passed 23 subjects: instead, he's got three national standard grades. You lot had better stop playing games with our children's schooling!"

If the meeting had been conducted by a rabbit in the headlights like Hepton, the tide might have turned. But with his indifference to the outcome, and knowing Hepton would be in the frame anyway, Pleasant pushed back and took back control. Didn't they realise their children might pass fewer subjects, but each subject would mean much more? Didn't they want their children to have real, transferable skills they could actually use in their careers? Didn't they want a government that took difficult decisions to secure their children's futures? If the audience didn't realise Pleasant's questions were rhetorical, his shouting was clue. The group was stunned: no one had dared speak to them like this before. Pleasant had mixed it up successfully to prevail, and the citizen consumers gave him some messaging he could pass on.

More revision please was the opening gambit to motivate the competitive instinct in children and their parents to defeat the new exams. *Enough revision thank you* was the pivot he chose to share with Hepton. If the new exams placed too much stress on children and their families, and this became too big an issue to close down, the government could make great store of how it listened and changed tack.

6

Hepton was staccato with overwork and looking to tick another box when Pleasant reported back the schooling fix he'd cooked up.

"Talk me through *More revision please* first. What's the sell to take minds off the latest schooling mess?"

"The sell is parents' vicarious competition through their children, in this case to pass these new exams. It also channels a sort of intellectual fitness. If we pitch it right we can get parents obsessed with getting their child over the line, and putting more pressure on teachers to make it happen. We need ultra-competitive parents to front the campaign, the sort whose children have conditional validation based on achievement. If the sell is pitched right it could ignite the step change in schooling achievement every government has been promising for decades."

"Competition's always popular in the Cabinet Office. But can it secure enough support?"

"It can if we pitch it right as a lifestyle choice. There's only a small calculated risk because we're in the second year of the new exams. Teachers and parents already know pass marks are going up, and there's even a bit more time to prepare."

"Give me the exit strategy if it all goes wrong."

"Enough revision thank you. If the polling about schooling stays stubbornly negative we say we're not apologising for our ambition, but we're a government who listens to feedback and therefore we're pausing the exams plan. We can cut curriculum content, but only at the last minute, so it produces a wave of relief in children and, more importantly, in their parents. That'll give us some sort of polling bounce back. And we can set the pass marks based on the public mood."

"I like it more now I can see the down slope."

"So, yes to the calculated risk on the up slope?"

"Would like to say yes, but it must be about effective positive messages. I'd need a sense of the campaign family's appeal. Time's against us, Pleasant; it might not be doable."

"It's all in hand, Hepton. I've got a family coming in for a breakfast chat tomorrow. One parent in academe, one self-made and running their own company, high achieving twins, a son and daughter the right ages."

"OK. We'll both get the credit if I can deliver on the sports grants and exams messaging in my next meeting with the Secretary of State. Where's your model family from?"

"That's why I'm sure it'll work, Hepton. They're from Domesboroughton."

7

Pleasant knew that Hepton needed to show he could perform when dumped on. His mother didn't disappoint when they met the family she'd sourced. Workaholic parents from divergent social backgrounds with fifteen year old twins, the son bookish and the daughter, Iphigenia, one of the most ruthlessly ambitious people both politicians had met of any age. Hepton's cautiousness transformed into real enthusiasm and the *More revision please* campaign launch was being filmed in a Domesboroughton mansion less than two weeks later.

The first edits of the filming set off the Whitehall rumour mill. Everyone wanted to see what was touted as certain to end the run of bad luck governments from all sides had had with British schooling policy. There was even talk of the family fronting the party's next general election campaign.

No one who saw the *More revision please* family in action doubted they would deliver enough support for the new exams to translate into electoral success. One scenario showed a mother supporting her son to prepare for his English literature exam. He was revising Macbeth and asked to be tested about Lady Macbeth's character development. Cut to the mother ordering her own Macbeth revision guide and working through the night with highlighters and a ruler in the family's large library. Then cut to testing her son and his frustration: "I just don't get it," and the panic in her eyes turning to excitement, with an animated light bulb heralding a great idea to ensure her son's exam success.

The next scene set up a puzzle, with numerous boxes of varying sizes being delivered to the front door. What was going on now? Viewers didn't have to wait long to find out she'd bought a portable stage and was fully costumed-up playing Lady Macbeth in her final scene to her audience of one. "He gets it now," she bellowed, taking a detour from the plot.

Showing a mother take to the stage to help their child revise English literature was certain to pack a punch with parents, but it was the exchange between father and daughter that really got Whitehall talking. Despite Daddy's stellar success in business, his performance played to his humble origins with his displays of deference to his singularly driven daughter. The clip focused on a series of e mails between them and his doomed attempts to book appointments in Iphigenia's diary to check she was happy with *more revision please.*

"Daddy, please, everything's changed since you were at school," kicked it off as Daddy abandoned his latest attempt to help Iphigenia with her science revision. (It didn't matter that he had a chemical engineering degree. *"Don't wheel out that one out again, Daddy."*) He offered to make her a snack of her choice when she wanted her next break, a victory only won after multiple exchanges between them. At first she told him off for emailing her to ask her if he could ask her a question, then for contacting her again to apologise.

"How can I revise properly if you keep interrupting me?"

Then he tried to be assertive. "Iphigenia, you need to take a break soon." A big mistake.

"Daddy, these exams are seriously challenging, so I'm taking them seriously. But you seem determined to interrupt my

concentration. Don't you care? Can't you wait until I contact you?"

Cue Iphigenia rubbing out and amending a mind map on one of the whiteboards in her room fading into Daddy typing ...parents...exams...HELP!... into his desktop computer and gloomily scrolling away. Then cut to a delivery van parking on the large drive of the family mansion, to create an air of mystery before the reveal. The caterers carried in a selection of brunch foods worthy of a luxury hotel. A picture of the feast in the state-of-the-art kitchen was e mailed to Iphigenia with a message, "Sorry to disturb. Refreshments ready when you want to take a break."

The clip ended with a reflection of Iphigenia in her laptop, eating while composing a final e mail to Daddy.

"Dear Daddy, I'm having to sacrifice even more of my revision time to send you this. I can only revise properly if I'm not disturbed! Why didn't you just send me a picture of the snacks you'd thrown together? Don't you know a picture speaks a thousand words? Why did you break my concentration by forcing me to read your message too? I was really looking forward to my next break, and the food looked edible, but you spoiled everything. How dare you disturb me to apologise for disturbing me. Do much better next time, or I won't be ready for my exams and it will all be your fault!"

The wave of government optimism produced by the *More revision please* family had dramatic consequences for Pleasant and his sponsor. Hepton was appointed as the new Secretary of State for Political know-how when his boss filled the gap from an unprecedented summer recess sacking at the Ministry for British Schools. And Pleasant filled Hepton's shoes as the new minister responsible for flipping policy flops.

8

It took less than a year for Pleasant to be elevated to the Cabinet. He took the purple patch of events from this time as proof that fate had destined him for greatness.

More revision please was launched at the start of September and quickly picked up the buzz of the new academic year, sweeping along enough children and parents to keep the media happy. By December it had acquired the qualities of a national campaign, with one newspaper exhorting parents to make this the best Christmas ever to give the school troops the rest and reward they deserved on their marathon campaign to spearhead the increase in schooling standards for the next generation. When other media outlets piled into the analogy, the government found itself achieving one nation levels of popularity and doubled down resources to build an inexorable mix of tension and excitement around the school troops in the home straight.

The New Year began to plan. January slowly ratcheted up the competitive spirit with a subtle change from autumn's *compete against yourself* to *compete to beat your friends*. A clever adaptation was banning schools from the usual targeting of children for revision at half term. Revision was still available, but it had to be booked by children themselves through a deliberately obscure online booking system; the type the government had lots of experience in getting wrong when the aim was access, but for once the inadequate design matched the strategy, to test children's clamour for more revision. When schools were fuller than ever with exam-aged children during half term, Hepton revealed to Pleasant that the PM had discussed possible dates for an early general election with the Cabinet.

Late winter and early spring were a charmed time for Pleasant. He'd become a minister when a campaign he'd created was increasing support for the government to unprecedented heights. He'd also inherited the role from Hepton, whose output was workaday but at least there was plenty of it. Pleasant was anything but overworked as a new junior minister, giving him time to network and think about his profile. Managing a re-brand before becoming a fixture in the Cabinet obsessed him until everyone's attention was pulled back to yet another schooling crisis.

Cracks began to emerge in late March. The Secretary of State for British Schools had kept a tight hold of the policy reigns to make sure her transfer from Political know-how wasn't the beginning of the end of her Cabinet career. It was her idea to ban the targeting of children for revision in February, which had had such a dramatically positive effect. She therefore decided to dictate a dramatic rise in mock exam grade boundaries to schools to sharpen feelings of imminent failure, and produce an even more desperate scramble for success. However, this deliberate blow was delivered to children at the same time that burnout had set in for many. Take up of Easter revision was sub-optimal to say the least, and the top reaches of the government spent the Easter break nurturing the delusion that this was the rest children needed before they did battle with the new exams.

Then an unexpected event beyond the government's control derailed the whole plan in weeks. The campaign twins turned sixteen in late April. Iphigenia acquired an agent and put her plan into action. She waited until the beginning of May, when a few stories about exam stress had made the inside pages. She then staged a meltdown on set while filming a motivational film the government had hurriedly scheduled to get the campaign back on track. The filming was meant to be sealed in the securest of bubbles, but Iphigenia's agent had two hacks from an anti-government national newspaper impersonating runners to record the whole performance. They propelled exam stress to the top of media agenda with their hatchet job on the government's exams campaign.

The battle of last orders was the headline exclusive the next day, with an account that got the nation talking.

What are we doing to our children, and at what cost? Yesterday, one of the twins fronting the government's exams campaign had had enough. You have probably seen how the twins have kept up with an assault course of demands from their school and their parents over the last eight months. They've transformed themselves into study machines to motivate children across the country not to blink first in the face of these tougher new exams. Yesterday, Iphigenia and her brother were revising late into the night, their parents seemingly messaging words of encouragement from another room.

What the government's hurriedly-scheduled film didn't show was the rigid timetable imposed on the twins by their parents' unrealistic expectations. Poor Iphigenia only asked for another snack after her last scheduled break in a day of revision due to end at 1am. It's revealing that her parents saw the argument

*that followed as two distinctly separate issues: asking for an
oatcake at midnight, after her scheduled break, and having the
time to eat the oatcake.*

*Before she left for rehab at an undisclosed location,
Iphigenia asked us to share with our readers her final take
away from the government's latest attempt to reset British
schooling.*

*"Don't let them tell you what you do is more important than
who you are. Find out what motivates you and dance to your
own tune. Don't be a sideshow in someone else's drama. Don't
be defined by an iffy exam."*

9

There was panic in government, and the panic wasn't
misplaced given the orchestration of their plan by Iphigenia and
her team. Iphigenia disappeared from view for six weeks to sit
her exams in an obscure rural boarding school used to shielding
the children of celebrities. Her team kept up the pressure,
issuing regular updates from a pre-recorded vlog about her
choreographed meltdown. The effect was to bring the
government's exams campaign crashing down to earth with
children, parents and the media aligning against them. But all
wasn't yet lost. That was why planned policy flip-flopping had
become a sub-section within the Ministry of Political know-
how. It was time for the exit strategy, the down slope.

And the reckoning. Even though the *Enough revision thank
you* campaign had been developed in parallel, government
insiders couldn't forgo one of their favourite pastimes; blame.
Bilateral meetings proliferated. No one divulged where they'd
been unless it was too risky not to do so. Hepton and Pleasant
kept each other superficially close. Pleasant knew Hepton had a
hotline to his former boss, trying to limit the damage at Schools.
They got on well, their conversations unforced, more like
thinking aloud. So when Hepton was reticent about a visit to
Schools that Pleasant knew had lasted most of a day, niceties
increased between them because little of any substance was
being shared. A week later Hepton was visibly crestfallen after
Cabinet, but sharing absolutely nothing. Perhaps Hepton was
passing blame further down the line to him, the person who'd
condensed this particular messaging out of the ether? Pleasant

was more chatty and avuncular than ever, a front for making the right move.

Then he received a call he couldn't even have hoped for.

"Don't you want Hepton Royd? What? Meeting the Prime Minister? Where? Sorry. When? Which entrance?"

His first visit to No. 10 on business was a memory Pleasant often returned to: that walk to a back entrance under cover of night, his trepidation turning into pure focus as time seemed to slow down, making him aware of the high stakes of every move. In the selective memory he preserved about his first one to one meeting with the PM, he had to play his cards carefully to avoid being the scapegoat for the whole exams catastrophe. The Prime Minister executed a speedy interrogation.

"Pleasant Drivelling, isn't it? You must have a good idea why I've asked you here? I understand you were Hepton Royd's PPS when he worked up *More revision please* and *Enough revision thank you* from that blasted focus group?"

Pleasant's head was in overdrive. So, Hepton hadn't hedged his role in the exams campaign? Probably fed into his workaholic narrative.

"Yes, Prime Minister. He has every confidence in the exit strategy."

"Who wouldn't if their name was on it? What I need to know is can we roll this out safely? Can we claw back the poll leads we've lost in the last two weeks?"

All right, he was the one who had worked this up with the focus group. He was the one who had shouted them down to get an exit strategy he could report back to Hepton to meet that unrealistic deadline. But he was only a PPS at the time, not formally part of the government. He appeared to be safely out of the frame, so this looked like an opportunity to share something with the PM he had kept back for a rainy day.

"I understand there was some dissent with the whole strategy in the focus group."

"Isn't that to be expected?"

"'I understand some of them took issue with more sudden changes to schooling standards. Tougher exams as a knee-jerk reaction to the last government's dabbling with schooling. A group of them creatively disposed of their meeting agendas at the end; all to a chorus of "watch this"."

"Watch what? I didn't ask you here to talk in riddles, Drivelling. If you've got something to say, say it."

"Some were ripped up, a few made paper aeroplanes: someone even scrunched their agenda into a ball and hit a slam dunk with it."

"What?!"

"I think they were meeting in a sports hall."

"I hope Hepton closed this down?"

"I don't think that was possible. But some thought *Enough revision thank you* might work if the government was humble enough to admit it went too far too quickly."

"This could take on a life of its own, Drivelling! Remember how schooling policy brought down the last government?!"

The PM was breaking his rule to keep the volume of the conversation in the room, but his micro rant was cathartic. He recovered his decorum and paused. Pleasant got in some final cover.

"I don't think *Enough revision thank you* would be in any danger without the campaign daughter's meltdown. No one could have foreseen that. And it's not certain we're in any real trouble. We've got an exit strategy. I'm up to date on all of this. I can support the Ministry for British Schools myself, if it helps."

Just in time Pleasant realised making it about himself wouldn't do with the Prime Minister, so he stopped talking. There was an even longer pause. Had he pitched things right? Then the meeting came to a sudden end.

"Thank you, Pleasant. This has helped. I didn't have a clear picture of that focus group before, and now I can see why. Keep your diary empty for tomorrow afternoon and make sure you confirm a number to be contacted on before you leave."

10

Pleasant Drivelling skulked out of the back of Downing Street and the next day he was walking up to the front door. He tried his best to stifle a grin to try to respect the process. Providence had elevated him out of the drudgery of junior ministerial ranks before any substantial new work took him away from managing his assault on the top. As expected, he was appointed as the new Secretary of State for Political know-how after the disgrace and untimely exit of his short-lived predecessor.

Pleasant simply stopped taking Hepton's calls. He gave no excuses, went radio silent having cleared his desk in their shared office after leaving Downing Street the night before, leaving an HR leaflet in the top drawer. Walking out of No. 10 after his five minute anointing, the new Secretary of State for Political know-how beamed at the cameras with a twinkle in his eye. He'd levered himself into the Cabinet ahead of schedule at the tender age of thirty-one. He was game on for political fame.

But he was soon brought down to earth. His first Cabinet meeting pitched Pleasant into a world of collective responsibility alien to his nature. He didn't know how to be part of a team. He cut off the Environmental Secretary and then the Home Secretary, all to prove he was the clever newbie who deserved his rapid promotion. His performance was met with scorn, especially from Hepton's old boss, who had annoyingly kept her job in the mini reshuffle. But the worst was still to come when full Cabinet ended. No one wanted to be seen with Pleasant over coffee. And conversation dried up in the groups he approached. Pleasant was so deflated when he left Downing Street; it was reported as a minor story inside one of the tabloids.

Pleasant got back to the Ministry of Political know-how and shut himself in his new office, folding his arms tightly and hugging his torso to get as close as he dared to the foetal position in his glass-walled goldfish bowl. He pretended to be deep in thought while staring at his computer in an attempt to throw his civil servants off the scent. Then someone marched into his office and changed his life.

11

"Ow do, Pleasant Driv'lin'? Ah'm yer special adviser at Political escape 'atch. Appointed by No. 10. Me name's 'ebden 'amble.

"Ebden Amble?"

"Nay lad. 'ebden 'amble. Call us Dinners; all me friends do. Ye wouldn't think ah'm from Doomsb'rton, would ye? Bang on me 'ead from me last bungee jump. Woke up in 'ospital soundin' like this. Unbelievable!"

Pleasant was uncharacteristically sensitive after his brutal Cabinet initiation. He might have reached another career milestone, but he was still wet behind the ears. He hadn't had time to schmooze and create a profile within his new ministry, where many must have suspected his hand in his predecessor's untimely downfall. And he'd almost been caught advertising his vulnerability by this rude stranger with a booming voice who showed no respect for protocol. Pleasant was so taken aback he forgot to engage his mouth in an angry return of serve. He paused and took in this giant of a man, built like the tallest of basketball players after a few years of the post-retirement good life. He was wearing the most utilitarian suit Pleasant had ever seen, more like a tailored boiler suit. The red mist had dissipated by the time Pleasant spoke.

"I've met with the PM twice in the last few days, and he said nothing about this job coming with a sitting special adviser."

"Course not! 'e wouldn't do detail like that in a one to one. That's f'r sussing out yer political nous. Ah spotted yer talents a while ago, Drivlin'. Kept me 'ead down waitin' f'r ye t' get this job. Me role's t' make sure yer ministry only passes on quality messagin'. Cut out the crap so no more rebounds, like with these bloody exams. Believe us; the PM's really got 'is eye on ye. Thinks ye can break away from the 'angers-on in t' Cabinet, but ye need me 'elp."

"I've got into the Cabinet in record time through my own ability alone. Why should I take advice from someone I've never even met before?"

"Ye don't remember us? Unbelievable! Check in with No.10 if ye don't trust 'is plan. But y'll be left in t' pack if 'e can't trust ye. And they'll 'ave ye."

Pleasant didn't say anything for nearly a minute, a new record. He was slightly losing his footing because Dinners was targeting his blind spot for credulity when he sensed getting something for nothing. He might as well hear Dinners out.

"I'm listening."

Dinners immediately switched to back to charm.

"Got a safe 'ouse f'r 'igh-ups in t' middle o' nowhere. Ah'll get pitches t' other side o' me one-way mirror. Ye don't 'ave t' break cover unless yer gonna go f'r it. Give us the weekend and ah'll set yer up as the new name in t' Cabinet."

Pleasant couldn't totally dismiss this ridiculous idea. Judging by this man's front, he might have some real power behind him. He could keep a low profile.

"Who else will be there?"

"Only thee be'ind t' mirror, 'an me in front. Ye can watch us sussin' out the pitches. Naff'ns won't even know yer there. 'ave ye got the guts t' jump in, Driv'lin'?"

Pleasant hesitated; taking in the swagger Dinners was planting as a first impression.

"Give me the address. What time should I get there?"

After the horror of his first Cabinet meeting, Pleasant was prepared to go off-piste.

12

Dinners gave Pleasant a map coordinate, a hat to wear from the motorway exit and an 11.30pm to 11.45pm Friday night arrival window. Pleasant left London early to make sure he arrived on time. The final approach was reassuringly through the narrowest of country lanes, screened by high hedges. He reached the designated spot at 11.16, which felt so isolated he took off his disguise.

Twenty-nine minutes later Dinners appeared on foot out of the darkness and gestured for Pleasant to follow him. Dinners took a sharp left and Pleasant found himself pulling into a gravel drive. Dinners stopped in front of an unfinished barn conversion and gestured for Pleasant to drive into a dilapidated wooden shed. Dinners followed switching on a dingy light, allowing Pleasant to take in the inauspicious surroundings.

"Ye don't 'ave t' stay in me 'ouse if yer not ready. Ye can sleep an' do yer thinkin' in 'ere. Looks like a dump, but it's five stars down those stairs. Four pitches booked in tomorro' t' raise yer profile. Hour each max, but ah'll call time if ah need t'. Ye can choose t' be with us, stay be'ind me mirror, or stay back 'ere if yer still not sure. Any one cuts it, ah'll invite 'em back on Sunda'. Any problems?"

Pleasant shook his head, suddenly feeling a lot more confident about the whole thing. Dinners seemed to appreciate the need to manage his risk.

13

Dinners had booked four pitches vying to raise Pleasant's profile. Pleasant decided to remain in his plush bunker, watching the pitches by camera until something was interesting enough to move closer to the action. The day got off to a very slow start. The first two pitches proposed different versions of Pleasant Drivelling the political innovator, with the public rallying behind him. The first pitch promised to make voting cool again through fresh eyes. Pleasant was invited to promote their campaign to make voting compulsory from the age of sixteen. Despite his safe vantage point Pleasant froze, remembering getting sand kicked in his face on a succession of beaches across three continents.

"Stop it there, tell them to get out," Pleasant shouted into Dinners' ear piece.

"I can give or take being called a libertarian, but I'm not putting my name to increasing the franchise."

Pleasant and Dinners then had an unexpected ninety minute break, but chose to remain in their separate bunkers.

The second presentation initially had more interest for Pleasant. A pressure group persuading the super-rich to fund difficult to justify new government initiatives could be onto something. Pleasant immediately saw the potential to fund an endless succession of publicity-hungry vanity projects, but pulled the plug after hearing a warning sign.

"Dinners, fully audited outcomes are not what I'm about at all. Tell them thank you, but no."

Two presentations down and there had been thin pickings for raising Pleasant's profile as a political innovator. Perhaps being a political influencer was Pleasant's best route to the top?

The next pitch had two actors expecting Dinners to believe their conceit that, without props but with interminable miming, they were working in a busy office they'd made into a home from home. This presentation lasted longer because it wasn't clear for a long time what they were pitching. The actors were in their own world, pointing every so often to a mime by the other and holding up a felt-tipped placard with their only comment - unbelievable. Dinners' response was nuanced at first. Rather than ask them what they were up to he stared in astonishment, occasionally turning to the hidden camera to look Pleasant in the eye. The actors were oblivious, and kept on with their heightened gestures in their imaginary world. Dinners' patience inevitably ran out.

"What the 'ell's goin' on?"

"Sorry, this is really new, but we can't see anyone ignoring the first sitting politician who openly uses product placement."

"What bloody products?" Dinners was annoyed.

"I thought the coffee maker Jemima endorsed was unbelievable. Jemima thought the foot massager I used at my desk was unbelievable. I thought the pin ball machine Jemima was playing was un…"

"GET THEM OUT OF HERE! NOW!!" Pleasant exploded, thinking how stupid he'd been to waste a day on this.

"Unbelievable. Ah get it now. A lot to think about," cut in Dinners as he walked them to the door.

14

After three failed pitches, and with no sense of irony, Pleasant was beginning to think that Dinners was all talk. He took minutes to calm down, and there was still a long wait until the final pitch of the day, but he didn't want a conversation with Dinners. This fool was going to be shown the door very soon.

Pleasant tuned in to the last pitch late to show he was annoyed. What he saw was Dinners having a pleasant conversation with a young woman with a bohemian vibe. His ruse to stress out Dinners clearly hadn't worked.

"You can get labelled by a label," was the first thing Pleasant heard.

"We offer our clients an image reset, not a makeover. We try to change one or two things dramatically for impact. We let the changes do the talking, that way you can get a wider range of people projecting onto the celebrity. I've brought some images to give you a sense of what we can do."

The woman proceeded to swipe through images on her tablet. The problem was that Pleasant couldn't see any of this through his camera.

"Can ye project yer thin telly on t' wall?"

The first set of images showed a ___ *days to disaster* neck tattoo, brandished by a political pundit who used non-permanent marker to update the number, which also allowed them to switch between political disasters.

"Bit 'ard t' change gear. Politics is nowt without U-turns." Dinners gestured to move on.

The next set of images showed a counter-intuitive fashion statement saving a flagging career. The sci-fi shoulder pads unleashed a flood of product endorsements, but Dinners wasn't interested.

"Can't wear owt that gets ye stuck in yer office door."

The final images showed a pop star's pivot into a successful music critic, helped by a haircut that definitely made an impression, though it was difficult to pin down why.

"'air's a good'n, can be changed easy." Pleasant expected the whiff of interest from Dinners regardless as the day's options ran out.

"Oo does the 'air?"

"A stylist who moonlights incognito from her day job on a TV sing-along. She does the star's hair and makeup because she's the most consistent stylist around. She's used to delivering a bespoke look, short notice. She's available tomorrow until 1. I can book her before I leave."

Dinners stared in the camera's direction.

"Go on. She can 'ave a go on me first, so me VIP can decide." A call confirmed the 11am booking, and the coast was soon clear.

"That's why ah volunteered meself t' go first. Ye don't even 'ave to break cover if yer still not up f'r it. But ye need a plan after what 'appened to 'epton. The Cabinet pack'll 'ave ye f'r breakfast. Ah think ye can go far in this game, an' the PM agrees with us, but ye need summat t' break free o' the rest of 'em. Ye need a profile t' command the stage, an' that's a good 'ead of 'air on ye, Pleasant-lad. Why not make it work f'r ye?"

Why not? Dinners was a persuasive protagonist. What did Pleasant have to lose?

15

The stylist arrived at 10.45 on Sunday morning. Pleasant had already decanted from his lair, sitting behind the one-way mirror to get a ringside seat for Dinners' image reset.

"You can give me a picture and/or a few words and I'll tell you what's possible for you."

"Ah'm thinking Roman emperor. 'appen Nero...but with an 'eart."

'Yes, that's doable. You're helped by your hair thinning. I can give you an arc of curls to frame your face. It'll take less than half an hour."

"Do it."

And do it she did, in silence with the concentration of a master artisan. Her focus cast a Zen-like calm on Dinners in the hot seat. He too couldn't afford to look ridiculous back at the office, but clearly realised he was in safe hands and manoeuvred his ego aside to allow her to work her magic. He even forgot to cast glances towards Pleasant on the other side of the mirror. Pleasant wasn't looking at Dinners anyway. Against his better judgement he was considering following Dinners into that chair, because he hadn't seen a more accomplished mastery of skill for a long time. He understood why Dinners gave completely positive feedback, something unheard of. Was he going to do this? Was he going to reveal he was here?

"She's 'avin' a break now, ready on the hour. Moment of truth, Driv'lin'. Are yer in or out?"

"I'm going to say in, as long as I get editorial control."

"Remember, she 'ates faffin' about. She likes 'er instructions up front."

"Someone that professional is going to be able to manage a feedback loop."

16

Pleasant made sure he was already in the chair when the maestro returned. Better no names: she was tied into her contract, but didn't want to disappoint her growing freelance demand. Pleasant was perturbed she didn't recognise him. But perhaps this was also part of the act to protect all concerned. At the back of the room Dinners had been put in no doubt that his special adviser role, whatever it was, was on the line if this went wrong. He was sat where Pleasant could keep an eye on him during his own image reset.

"I thought I could make more of the height I've got on top. Could you accentuate it?"

"Yes, I can see that. Do you want much of a flick back when you shake your head? It could add to overall the effect given the thickness of your hair."

"A bit of a flick back, why not, but nothing like a mullet. More like a horse's mane. Do you understand?"

"Anything else before I start?"

"Nothing for now."

"I'm not being rude, but I need to conceptualise at the start. Trust me, I don't get disappointed customers."

"All I can say is I'll try, but I'm not in showbiz. I need to stand out and blend in at the same time."

"OK. Just keep the comments to a minimum. I'm sure there won't be a problem when you see how I work."

That was a cue for Pleasant to stop talking and let the styling begin.

"You must understand I'm an elected public official. I'm only here by consent, and I can't take that consent for granted. I've got to be sure the public has confidence in my words and in my actions ... and in my appearance. I've been entrusted as a steward to ..."

"I've got to leave at 1. Can we start?"

"Yes, start now." Pleasant rolled his eyes in the mirror to get Dinners' attention as he gave the final go ahead for his image reset. He didn't care if she saw him. It would remind her of his high expectations.

And so began what unexpectedly became the most defining episode in Pleasant Drivelling's political career to date. The circumstances conspired to surface parts of his character he usually kept on a tighter lead. Pleasant could easily keep an eye on Dinners from his chair, but didn't feel the need to. Dinners was nicely in abeyance in the last chance saloon. This was a one to one between Pleasant and a hairdresser here to do his bidding: no need for charm or to limit his input.

"Still too long here! Shorter than that! Blend it more! Don't take any more off there!"

The shouting began, and it quickly became a self-fulfilling prophesy. The artisan maintained her professionalism, saying nothing at all to avoid adding fuel to the fire while working demonstratively more slowly and methodically, to show rather than say she was listening.

But Pleasant wanted continuous validation, and this set him off even more.

"Just stop it right there. Are you listening to me?"

Pleasant abruptly moved his head to one side to make her stop and take more instructions.

"This is my image; my reputation is at stake here. I want this job finished to my satisfaction. Is that clear?!"

Pleasant was suddenly having his head forced down. He couldn't break free. He was in mild shock, and time seemed to stand still. When released he took a few seconds to raise his head to look in the mirror for his assailant. He couldn't see her anywhere, even when he turned around to scan the room. She must have gone. Feeling out of danger, he turned to face the mirror again, and relaxed enough to take in his new image. He immediately tensed up again.

What he noticed first was Dinners brandishing hair clippers and then – with a sharp intake of breath – the result. Pleasant did indeed have his horse-like mane, but his head was shaved on both sides.

"What's she done to me?"

"Wasn't 'er. Trust us, ah've saved ye. Ye were 'eadin' f'r a daytime telly look, all wrong. Now ye can punk out yer profile. Cabinet meetin' in two days. If ye can carry this off, it'll make ye."

Pleasant couldn't speak for a while, paralysed by fear. What had just happened broke all the rules, yet at the same time the pendulum seemed to have swung in Dinners' favour.

"Shall ah shave off the middle? Ye can try n' stay under the radar with a buzz cut."

With this Dinners gestured to shave off the peak, putting Pleasant on the spot to choose between relative safety and the ego trip of his life.

Pleasant made the obvious choice.

17

"Leave it for now. I've got a day to experiment with it. I'll try out some hair products and decide what to do before Tuesday."

Pleasant tried to be calm, but his reflection in the mirror jolted him back to reality.

"How can I get back to London in this state?"

"Ah thought ye were goin' for it? Jump in t' deep end. Show 'em what yer made of."

"Not an option." After what had just happened, Pleasant baulked at the idea.

"Cancel all my appointments for tomorrow. Have you got a hat or something with a hood?"

"Nowt like that in the 'ouse. Drive like the clappers. Wait 'till dark if it 'elps."

"Yes, I'll wait until later. Gives you time to find me something to cover this up."

"Ah told ye ah've got nowt 'ere. Yer a bloody lightweight, Driv'lin'!"

Dinners' contempt came out of nowhere and cemented his new advantage. Pleasant couldn't handle a row in this state. He needed to get away from Dinners, and from what he'd just done.

Pleasant was aware of being in and observing his strop at the same time. Running back to his room, packing in seconds, panicking looking for his keys, almost scratching the car door in his eagerness to get in. Then a stroke of luck. He'd forgotten the hat that Dinners had given him for the outward journey, which he'd left in the car. It looked ridiculous, but fitted completely over the meal Dinners had made of his hair. It helped Pleasant steady his latest wobble.

Pleasant holed himself up in his flat, ordering a range of hair products on next day delivery. First he thinned the offender, brushing it both sides, then all to one side, then the other. Although Dinners had cleared his diary he made calls with each style, studying himself in the mirror and trying for a sense of someone the other side of the table from this very unusual Secretary of State. With a name like Drivelling and now this hair! By Monday evening Pleasant was at a new level of despair. He even considered bringing forward his annual visit to his father. Playing truant from Cabinet could spare him being dragged around another golf course, but he couldn't survive the endless chatter in this state!

At 9pm he used hair gel to spike it up so he could stare the full implications of his new look squarely in the face. He'd been ignoring Dinners all day, but now took a call. No, he hadn't shaved it off yet. No, he wasn't definitely going to keep it. He tried to sound assertive, but when Dinners reminded him he had to break cover tomorrow morning, his voice trembled and he ended the call.

If the day had been bad, the next few hours were on another level altogether. He only slept for a couple of hours, after a shower and a few whiskeys. He woke up at 3.22 feeling dishevelled, and stared from his bed at the hair clippers that represented his other nuclear option. His mind wandered back to Dinners. Dinners had shaved him into a singular future. Perhaps Dinners was a much more insightful character than he realised? Perhaps he could see what others couldn't see? Pleasant decided to put off his final decision until the hour from 6 to 7am. This allowed him to fall asleep, letting his subconscious continue evaluating.

He woke up feeling much fresher, showered, got a coffee and sat in front of the mirror at 6.23 feeling unhurried. The lack of hair products added clarity. He could spin a tale about a sponsored haircut for charity. Dinners could retro fit a suitable narrative. He held the hair clippers, switched on, over his head – and made his decision. He was going to go for it! Dinners was right. It could make him! He called Dinners to get out a story about charity – nothing the Secretary of State can really talk about; needs to be kept private so he can carry on volunteering – and got ready to leave.

18

Pleasant was generally self-regarding in front of cameras. It sometimes cost him not paying enough attention to the people around him. But today it helped. He walked up Downing Street with his new haircut blocking out journalists' reactions. An overly serious expression greeted the few incredulous faces he caught sight of. He reached a relative safety when he entered No. 10. The staff didn't react, bricked in behind their roles. He took his seat in Cabinet, and it wasn't that different to his first traumatic meeting. His colleagues still only paid him enough attention to be seen to ignore him. The Prime Minister was the exception. He shot glances across the table at him, and then succumbed to a smile.

Cabinet business took Pleasant's mind off his predicament. Luckily, Political know-how wasn't on the agenda today. He felt a wave of bravery before coffee break, but then spent most of it in the toilet avoiding people. He left wishing he had bit the bullet of a one to one conversation, and faced a mob of journalists shouting his name, bursting out in a self-satisfied grin as he ostentatiously pretended they weren't there. If anything, this walk felt longer: he started to feel fear on his horizon again, but then...

"Get in, Pleasant." Dinners beckoned from the back seat of his ministerial car.

"Yer doin' great, minister."

"Do you think so?"

"Ah've 'eard the press are blown away with ye. They know not to pry so ye can keep up yer volunrt'y work!"

For the driver's ear. "I'm relieved. I'd have hated this sponsored haircut to end my association with them."

Pleasant glided through the rest of the day. Yes, he faced amused smiles, but there was a general benevolence in them. Westminster didn't often see senior government ministers setting such a worthy example. Dinners had anticipated things brilliantly, diverting all his calls so he was not available for comment, and could only be seen doing his job. He arrived back home late and got a text from Dinners.

TURN TELLY ON. NOW!

Pleasant tuned in and walked through a portal into his future. *Leading from the front of this house* was the headline in the biggest selling tabloid, with a profile shot of Pleasant on the House of Commons terrace, pretending he was listening to the awestruck minions vying to speak with him. Within forty-eight hours Dinners had manufactured a narrative so convincing, Pleasant actually enjoyed his interview with a broadsheet features editor. Everyone wanted to meet the new celebrity politician, but politely kept to the business at hand, respecting someone who set the best of examples. At his next Cabinet meeting Pleasant still felt like an outsider, but now in good way. His colleagues now wanted to be associated with him, and he effortlessly flipped from a Cabinet beta to the top ranked alpha.

Dinners aggressively peppered Pleasant's new profile into the general discourse. Within a month *front of house* internet searches were trending Pleasant's selfless deeds to an ever widening fan base. And when he pulled off a career high chat show appearance as *the politician with some front* – with no mention of Pleasant or Drivelling at all – Dinners upped the ante. Why not front out a proper reset?

Why not? Dinners was right. He should have trusted Dinners all along. He was in safe hands, the coolest member of the Cabinet, even a centre of gravity separate from the PM himself. At last, a Secretary of State for Political know-how ready to take his rightful place at the front of the stage.

I'll make the tea

1

At the Ministry for British Schools Valentine Vaklerner had begun taking notes for the memoirs he intended to write after Prime Minister Front sacked him. Every day something excited the junior schooling advisers in the open office space. Valentine had a ringside seat through the glass wall of his office, and had wound his office politics bingo card back to the era of silent films, looking for predictable actions: tripping on the carpet in the rush to meet a deadline; standing bolt upright in a light bulb moment; a group jostling each other around a desk. Mercifully, most of the drama blew itself out. A memorable exception was the week one of them got a gig for Cosmina Blame as a first time TV newspaper reviewer after a late cancellation.

This marked the end of Cosmina's forays going solo front of house. It went without saying she would weave in some of their work regardless of the stories being reviewed. She was on later that same day, and was mobbed by office sycophants hoping their silo of innovation might get a mention. Valentine won another full house on his bingo card and added a new box: tantrums. Cosmina had lost her temper with the chorus of requests flying her way. Valentine called home with apologies for missing dinner, ordered a take away and settled into his office home from home for the evening. He knew that, apart from Sundays, a group of junior schooling advisers lived their best social lives in the office until late. The numbers glued to tonight's newspaper review were bound to be large. Few would want to be away from the office the moment a fresh jockeying for position began.

In the event, Cosmina didn't have to twist the discourse to include schooling. A piece of investigative journalism by a regional daily had been picked up by one of the national broadsheets. One of the news networks had been tipped off about yet another schooling scandal, and the last minute newspaper review vacancy was a set up to get comment from someone inside the schooling policy bubble. The trigger was a punch up between two parents at a secondary school gate that had gone viral on social media. The extension of the government-backed schooling lottery to secondary-aged children was the ultimate cause, and had set off the usual chain of unintended consequences that needed fire fighting.

2

A few months earlier Spads had returned from one of his meetings with the PM with the green light to allow parents of secondary-aged children to trade in their school complaints for entry to an expanded schooling lottery, now with ten annual winners and the same accompanying incentives. Unfortunately, a tendency soon emerged for some secondary school children to become practised school anti-heroes in their *I want better schooling* sweatshirts. Teachers and other children weren't safe. Some schools responded by overriding the national uniform policy, and banning the sweatshirts for instigating disorder. This soon stopped after two leading schools failed snap inspections for falling below minimum standards. School leaders were chastened, and reverted to covering up the bullying epidemic as best they could to keep under the Ministry's radar.

The Ministry kept its focus on the narrowest of metrics to claim it was doing a good job. It pointed to significant increases in parental satisfaction with schooling, evidenced by a steep increase in complaint resolution. This metric glossed over a very different reality. Most parents responded to bullying by lottery entrants by complaining to the school only to trade in their complaint to get their own child into the lottery. There ensued a war of all against all within schools, with lottery entrants attending school mainly to maintain or improve their position in the hierarchy. In parallel, the pushiest parents cut out the middle man: further school complaints were prohibited after trade in, so they took out their beef directly with other parents beyond the school gates.

This was the context of the social media frenzy over the fight between two parents whose daughters were vying to be top alpha in their school. Nine days later two journalists had identified disturbing patterns of child and parent behaviour that spanned region and socio-economic group. Cosmina left the Ministry conspicuously early wearing a cloak of false modesty draped over the triumphalist office culture she presided over. She was sent tomorrow's front pages just after 9.45pm; skim read a few but paid most attention to how she would weave in schooling hacks. The network withheld the front page exclusive from the reviewers until 10.22pm to set the trap.

Cosmina was unfazed. She relished the opportunity to communicate her mission to the widest possible audience. And she had full confidence in her tool kit of love-bombing, patronising and kicking down.

3

"And we're fortunate to have the political commentator Beverley Elbie and Cosmina Blame, a senior special adviser at the Ministry for British Schools, with us tonight. There's no obvious lead story in tomorrow's papers. We've got *Calls to make new homes cosier, Fear of schooling meltdown, Outrage over..., Fury at....* But let's start with *Could British robots run on fish and chips?* Beverley, the answer seems to be no."

Cosmina was helped by initially going second, and she was glad she'd told the acting senior junior schooling adviser to shut up and get out of her office earlier that morning, giving her time to read the article about listening he had brought her to curry favour. She still thought listening was overrated, but it could help her use the preceding comment to work out the newspaper review dynamic. She assumed her fellow newspaper reviewer needed to be pacified, while a more trenchant approach would put the news presenter in her place.

Then the order reversed, as expected.

"Now we turn to the headline *Fear of schooling meltdown.* Cosmina Blame might be able to shed some light on this exclusive investigation revealing a wave of bullying breaking out inside and outside of the nation's schools. Cosmina, they're highlighting a significant rise in bullying within schools that's spilling out onto the streets, and even involving parents. They're claiming the government has stoked a crisis by linking schooling to gambling. You're inside the Ministry for British Schools. Have they got it wrong?"

"If I might say so, Abby, I think your intro misrepresents the real situation. We've finally got a government prepared to give schooling a long overdue reset."

"I'm sure we can all agree that schooling isn't perfect, Cosmina, but can we focus on the antisocial behaviour epidemic described in this article? They place it firmly at the door of the government's decision to set up a lottery for school places, allowing school children to wear slogans that are undermining school discipline, and creating conflict between parents outside school gates. These are serious claims."

Cosmina wasn't flustered. This was her area of expertise.

"Either you simply don't understand or you're choosing to ignore the bigger picture, Abby."

"Gabby."

"Believe me, we're only at the start of root and branch change to schooling that's going to be AMAZING."

Beverley wasn't impressed. "Cosmina, behaviour's becoming unrecognisable NOW, ON THIS GOVERNMENT'S WATCH! This paper's found spikes in school bullying and parents losing the plot in all regions. Yes, schooling's been a political football for years, but this looks like a bad situation falling off a cliff!"

Cosmina quickly amended her risk assessment.

"You're getting the wrong end of the stick, Bev."

Now playing up to Gabby in an obsequious tone.

"I know your viewers would appreciate a bit more detail about how we are burning the midnight oil to scale the heights and go the extra mile for the good of all – so I'll give you an example. School places have been a lottery for decades. This government is the first to be honest about it. So we've made our own lottery, yes, to give a few children a fresh start. But, more importantly, we're motivating all the entrants – and their parents – to hope for better, and move away from the complaints culture our schools have been mired in."

Gabby wasn't pacified. "Stirring words and an admirable ambition, Cosmina, but could you address the point? If schools aren't safe and it's spilling out onto the streets, whatever the intentions, isn't this really the most dangerous decline in schooling standards yet?"

Cosmina was used to a level of autonomy where such challenge was unheard of. There was no way she was going to appear defensive in front of these two, especially not on live TV. So she decided to finish on a positivist flourish, regardless of what had and had not been placed in the public domain.

"We've had to start working with schooling as it is. That's why we've got this real buzz building around the brand new schooling lottery. But this is only the start. Doesn't everyone want schools to take care of all the learning a child needs? Of course they do. That's why we're putting families at the centre of everything. We're writing a word perfect curriculum, abolishing exams and simplifying assessment so teachers can't get it wrong any more. Children will get all of the schooling they need during the school day, so no need for the stress of homework, and ultimately no need for much studying at university to let children concentrate on their social lives. Bullying? Of course school behaviour's going to be sorted out too. When we're finished, British schooling won't be recognisable!"

"Big changes and big implications. Beverley, we're nearly out of time. Any final comments?"

"Nothing to add other than that I'm speechless."

Cosmina felt she had made her point.

4

Cosmina's triumphant return to base the next morning was complicated. The junior advisers buzzed around her as usual, saying and believing she had "done great". She lingered in the open office longer than Valentine liked from his vantage point, but he enjoyed knowing what was coming next. Spads appeared on cue, looking shaky after a dose of telephone wrath from the PM, followed up quickly by a vicarious apology through the PM's chief special adviser to keep the messages mixed and the underlings pliant. While Hebden Hamble was on the phone to a confused Spads, Valentine was getting his own telling-off from the PM, so knew what was coming. Would Spads have the guts to set a boundary with his deputy?

The answer appeared to be no. Cosmina was out conducting in the open office within the hour, and Spads was seen outside the building smoking a cigarette. Nobody knew he smoked. Valentine was under strict instructions from Front to make sure Cosmina Blame understood her role was exclusively behind the scenes from now on.

"I'll make the tea," offered a relieved Spads when Valentine agreed to lead a second attempt to carry out the PM's high-decibel order. Here was another job the lead senior adviser for schooling hacks wasn't up to. Valentine would touch his right temple when it was safe for Spads to enter.

What stayed with Valentine about this interaction were Cosmina's eyes. When he called over to her in the open office to meet him "now, it's quite urgent," her contempt was unfiltered. He was used to his seniority being no haven at the Ministry, but her glint of surprise which instantly morphed into a steely stare put him on edge. Cosmina resumed the conversation she was having about anti-bullying strategies, walked slowly back to her office and shut the door.

Valentine was starting to sympathise with Spads' hesitancy. Did he have to accept the ignominy of crossing the open office to speak to his special adviser's deputy? He decided to wait things out, but still felt a slight panic when Cosmina left her office nearly ten minutes later, marching in his direction carrying a folder stuffed with paperwork.

Valentine read Cosmina's incredulity correctly as he informed her that all public-facing statements about schooling had to come through the PM, Spads or himself. The order he used reflected the real hierarchy of schooling policy, but was also a ruse to sugar the pill for Cosmina about boundaries on her role. She was the key gatekeeper for all research about schooling for the Ministry and therefore the government. In front-facing politics U-turns were becoming the norm, but they still had to be managed carefully. He, Spads and the PM didn't want such limitations on her work. They relied on her can-do thinking, needed her to feel free to change her mind as many times as needed to stay on top of the moving target of the schooling revolution they were embarked on.

Cosmina was looking teary. Was it working? Sort of. The tears were anger. She knew all of this already. She'd been in a pivotal discussion about the no physical contact rule in schools, which he had rudely interrupted. She had all of the research here, but wouldn't share it yet because there were three very different strategies she was still evaluating. She'd wasted enough time on this nonsense. It was taking her away from making sense of the research. She left without waiting for an answer, almost knocking over a civil servant carrying three mugs of tea to a jumpy Spads sitting at a desk near Valentine's door.

"How did she react?"

"I think she got the message, but could I give you a bit of advice, Spads?"

"Anything. Thank you, thank you."

"Never forget. Cosmina's always interviewing us."

5

The cyclical nature of office politics quietened things down for Valentine over the next few weeks. Spads accepted his suggestion to remove the redraft limit on the cracking new schooling curriculum, which was chipping away at some of the most rushed content. Even the wave of secondary school bullying caused by the government's new schooling lottery reached a kind of herd immunity with more entrants, and calmed down.

Years before Valentine had watched a drama documentary about Bletchley Park that was sequenced with such immediacy he escaped from hindsight for a split second, and had a fleeting sense of the crisis on the home front during the Battle of the Atlantic. He called on this memory to help him move his foresight about the schooling disaster ahead to the back of his mind. He wallowed in the respite, spending a summery early autumn pretending he was more observer than participant in this unprecedented schooling project.

He was also helped by Spads and Cosmina spending more time out of the office, touring schools across the country on a fact-finding mission. Spads had wanted the tour to be simultaneous PR for the schooling revolution, something akin to an update of a Tudor royal progress. It beggared belief how quickly he'd forgotten the media gymnastics needed after Cosmina's last public outing.

Spads was only at ease talking about opportunities and potentialities with Cosmina. They would chatter away in the collaboration amphitheatre, forgetting anyone else was there. There was no way of knowing how the two of them would behave together in the wider world, so Valentine tried to impress on Spads that the visits needed to stay completely under the radar.

Valentine only received one nasty surprise during the tour, a letter of complaint from an under-funded school in the far north that had brought out Spads' London-centric snobbery. He and Cosmina had just had a working lunch with the governing body in the headteacher's office. Spads had left the room while finishing an apple, and threw the apple core on the single piece of carpet in the whole dilapidated building.

While we could have had clearer signage for the litter bin, and have since rectified the issue, our staff at reception are always on hand to respond to visitors' requests. The headteacher was clearly incensed but aware of her audience, mindful of the range of repercussions possible for putting her head too far above the parapet.

Valentine viewed the incident with a much simpler interpretation.

6

The relative calm at the Ministry ended suddenly with a call from No.10. One of Hebden Hamble's assistants informed Valentine that a film crew had been hired for next week, and he was booked in on Wednesday at 3.30pm for a short closing scene to round off the presentation of the government's new anti-bullying schooling initiative. The call ended as he was asking what the initiative was.

A transformed Spads and Cosmina were already back at the Ministry when Valentine arrived the next morning. Gone was the hint of grunge that used to advertise their status as radical thinkers. They looked like they'd appointed personal shoppers. Spads' garb suggested an update of the Edwardian motorist, while Cosmina was channelling nuclear bunker command with accessories. Whatever they had shared with the junior schooling hackers had had a dramatic effect. They were managing the crowd like film stars but, when Spads realised his minister had sneaked in, he made a beeline for Valentine's office.

Spads entered quickly after a peremptory knock on the office door.

"Valentine, I need to speak to you urgently. We've only got two months until the new schooling lottery draw and the preview of the new curriculum on Christmas Eve."

"How was the tour, Spads? Has Cosmina taken to her new role?"

"I don't want to be rude, Valentine. I'm taking an urgent call in fifteen minutes, so I've got to cut to the chase. I've met with the PM and he wants to max out schooling initiatives to fit in with a much bigger Christmas launch. We've been given access to No.10's best modellers, and it's helped us see we've got the space to insert a behavioural idea we've developed which we're going to launch here at the Ministry in a fortnight. The content's embargoed to maximise impact. You've got a scene at the end of next week's filming. You'll get your lines on the day."

Valentine was used to more of a filter on Spads' ego in their meetings. The contrast from the last time they had met was unsettling.

"But I'm the Minister for British Schools, Spads. Do you know what that means?"

"Yes, we need you to rubber stamp the plan. Look, Valentine, these are orders from No. 10. The PM's hooked me up with his top special adviser to help us out. I'd see this as an opportunity if I was you."

"What *can* you tell me about this latest inspired initiative, Spads?"

Valentine's sarcasm passed Spads by.

"It was playtime at a secondary school in Reading that gave us the idea. The headteacher loaned us his office for the rest of the day. We had to cancel our meeting with the school parliament to seize the moment. I even penned a short speech he read to the children explaining that important people sometimes had to change their plans at short notice. They'd find this out if they grew up to be important people themselves. To cut a long story short, we left that school with a piece of paper that's going to go down in schooling history!"

It wasn't worth another go. Spads was lost in his own epic.

"Can I go now?"

Then Minister for British Schools walked out of his own office without waiting for a response.

7

Valentine was none the wiser after filming his twenty second scene for the presentation taking place today in his own ministry, with a live stream to No.10. With two hours to go, he found the atmosphere unbearable. He left the building to go for a long walk with his phone switched off. When he returned, the open office space had been transformed by the velvet curtains screening the mocked-up theatre stage that was the hottest ticket in Whitehall.

The room was packed, they were standing at the back, and there was only one vacant seat – next to his. The seat stayed vacant as the scheduled start time came and went. Then there were signs something was happening behind the curtains. A knocked over microphone. Probably Spads. "LEAN FORWARD INTO THE LECTERN!" Cosmina's authoritarian default. A bottle of water then broke free from under the heavy curtains with a force suggesting it must have been kicked. It bounced and hit the acting senior junior adviser, who held it up like a prize with an inane wave back to the audience. Then a giant of a man landed on the vacant seat, jolting Valentine to one side without any acknowledgement.

The Cabinet perceived Hebden "Dinners" Hamble as a pervasive eminence grise at No.10. He rarely talked to anyone in open forum, certainly not them. Valentine thought he'd once heard Dinners shouting in a side room, but Front was also in there so he couldn't be sure. Now he was sat next to the government's top special adviser who was ignoring him, not even pretending to look at his phone. The lights suddenly went out. Someone in events had done their homework because it was very dark indeed. Nothing seemed to be happening just long enough to think something had gone wrong: no it hadn't, as he recoiled from the booming melodramatic music, cut across by a distorted techno beat. Then an amplified voice cut through the din, rattling off the latest schooling transformation agenda.

"We are already a game changer in our first Whitehall project at the Ministry for British Schools."

"First an' bloody last."

"The evil dragon of exams HAS BEEN SLAIN!"

"So bairns can't remember owt."

"A curriculum match fit for the future."

"Aye, if the future's a soddin' stone age."

"Precision-engineered assessment."

"Copied out today's load o' rubbish yet?"

"A teaching community trained directly by us to meet our new national standard to lead the world."

"This mob couldn't lead a ********************!"

Valentine was getting a flowery version of his own critique from the Prime Minister's chief special adviser! What was going on now? He certainly wasn't going to acknowledge any of Dinners' comments, which seemed quiet enough for only him to hear. He felt like he'd been placed in a stress position.

Spads and Cosmina had taken no chances with the ticket allocation. Despite the room being too cold from the building's air flow system, and the lower lumbar problems being created by its office chairs, the audience fizzed in anticipation of a new level of cool. The stage was hit by a piercing light and, as eyes adjusted, Spads' figure became visible behind a lectern as the curtains opened. During his time at the Ministry for British Schools, Valentine had observed Spads making less and less use of his talent for improvisation. Cosmina was standing six feet to the side holding a pack of cue cards. They stood there motionless for so long, some in the audience started looking at their phones. Valentine wondered if some of them were online shopping, adding fake monocles, breeches, combat boots and concrete jewellery to online checkouts to emulate the political influencers on the stage.

Spads finally spoke.

"Steady yourselves, fellow visionaries and innovators. Prepare yourselves, for what you are about to witness is a...," Cosmina handed Spads a new card, "...jump..." Spads jumped to one side and nearly fell over. Another new card, "... in human consciousness, the biggest game changer during this revolutionary time in our schools. We are going to give you a preview of a step change to a fast forwarded future for our schools. When you are watching our film, think about how we intend to get there, how we can solve such a basic problem which no one has thought to address like this before." Another card. "Lights." Darkness again. Then a long pause. "Prepare so be amazed." They must have forgotten Spads would be in darkness too. Perhaps he should have learned this line.

"Do us a favour. Can ye manage a nice runnin' ju...," but Valentine was tuning out of the commentary in his ear. He needed to give the film his full attention, because he was at the end of it endorsing whatever it was going to reveal. The lines they had given him were truisms that gave nothing away. They were capable of retrofitting anything to his words.

8

Valentine's first impression of the film was its slick production. The camera floated high above an urban landscape, and descended through broken clouds to happen upon a blurred open space with indistinct figures and movement. All of this in silence, then the camera descended to ground level with the sound of children playing football introduced in sync with the scene coming into focus. The camera glided closer to reveal two teams of secondary-aged girls and boys living in the moment inside their competitive game. The synthesis of drama school and football academy in the children was flawless: the game stayed centre stage for some time, allowing viewers to take in the attacks, tackles, counter attacks and fouls, and the damage done to school uniforms.

Then through the middle of the game an approaching adult came into view. The teacher on duty with *ON DUTY* helpfully written on the back of his high visibility jacket. The sound of an adult voice, but no distinct words. The game continuing until a whistle was heard, the teacher pointing at a *NO PHYSICAL CONTACT* sign. Children remonstrating about the game, the teacher pointing again at the sign and writing something, presumably names, in his pad.

The teacher departed, and a full contact game started as before. The sound of the whistle from the near distance. No effect. The whistle again, and cut to the teacher on duty with steam coming out of his ears. Cut back to the game, which only stopped because the ball was kicked to the far end of the playground. The camera followed a child running to retrieve the ball from near the teacher's feet. The child looked up and saw the teacher headless with fizzing wires emanating from his neck. What was going on now? Perhaps the robot was symbolic, but you couldn't be sure. More confusion. The child wasn't fazed, retrieved the ball and ran back to the group. The game began again, as physical as ever. The sound of a bell ended the game, with the children running wildly into the building, jostling each other with no regard for the no physical contact rule.

9

The camera took off again, up through the clouds and speeding across the metropolis. It allowed Valentine to dial down his intense concentration, but he became aware of being on edge, taking shallow breaths. He glanced along the front row and saw invitees and junior advisers lapping it all up. The acting senior junior adviser looked in raptures. He tried to galvanise himself to cast off a sinking feeling, and picked up some Beethoven.

Everyone was being kept on their toes with the camera alighting on the Palace of Westminster as a backdrop to a montage summarising the mechanics of legislative change: a green paper, a white paper, MPs and peers debating, a committee meeting, more debates. A quill pen signing something with a flourish, followed by a lightning bolt: the music abruptly stopped.

We were back in the same playground, now with a new teacher *ON DUTY* scanning the group of children obscured in the distance. A sense of movement as the camera slowly approached the group and then stopped, still at a distance. Back to the teacher smiling pleasantly at the group, jumping to a thermal imaging screen tracking the children with visual alerts flashing on and quickly off. What was triggering the alerts? Presumably physical contact.

With a sense of dread Valentine knew better than to expect the teacher was tracking the children with some sort of scanner. Of course, she was the scanner. Cut to negative and positive behaviour points frenetically scrolling upwards on the school's IT system. What was going on now?

Valentine had been mentally holding onto a rock face by his fingertips, trying to work out what he was going to endorse at the end of the film. He felt his grip failing when he saw the next scene. Cut to the children in the near distance playing football. No, not playing football. Dancing the playing of football. Uniforms pristine. No physical contact taking place, but a girl executed a perfectly choreographed dive to get the imaginary ball. Did he see that right? Had she bounced off the tarmac? She got up unruffled, with no damage to her uniform. Five seconds later a boy bounced off the floor unscathed. Perhaps they'd lined the floor with grey gym mats? Then the game suddenly ended, with the bell sounding and the children walking in silent physically-distanced single file into the building for their lessons.

Valentine felt lost in the foothills of panic when he saw himself sitting on the edge of a desk with the vaguest smile to instil government confidence in whatever the film had introduced.

"We can all agree that children's safety is directly linked to their learning. Now we have the policies to guarantee both." And the room was abruptly cast into darkness. They'd cut him right back to two lines!

When the lights came on again, Spads and Cosmina were sitting in armchairs on the stage looking very smug indeed.

"Spads does like his comfy armchairs," Valentine thought. "Hope these geniuses realise they've got a lot to explain."

10

The next segment replaced the expensive production values of the film with a no-frills chat between Spads and Cosmina. They'd mercifully realised that attention-grabbing riddles now had to give way to a more regular style of presentation, but they'd tweaked the format to maintain control. Spads chunked the historic changes ahead, and Cosmina interjected with the only questions allowed to keep Spads' clarifications on-message.

"Fellow stakeholders, who could disagree with our minister? When children are 100% safe they can concentrate 100% on their learning. Please forgive us our conceit. We're not proposing replacing teachers with robots. Absolutely not ... yet. The new behaviour strand in our schooling revolution will guarantee safety for all by using that under celebrated British value, the rule of law."

Spads paused for effect "... We will support older children to concentrate on their learning by treating school bullying as a criminal offence."

"From what age?" Cosmina asked on behalf of the audience.

"From the age of twelve. Children reach criminal responsibility at the age of ten. We reckon they need two years to transition to no physical contact at all at school."

"AMAZING! What about PE in secondary schools? Will contact sports be allowed?"

"Remember, contact sports will be allowed for children up to the age of eleven. But you're right; we expect children will learn to steer clear of a criminal record by giving up all contact sport inside school by their twelfth birthday."

Someone chipped in from the back of the room. "Isn't school bullying much more than children bumping into each other? And what if someone wants to give their best friend a hug?"

The next couple of minutes were a bit of a blur. Spads was suddenly alone on the stage, looking like an abandoned ventriloquist's dummy. Cosmina was nowhere to be seen, but there was a commotion at the back. Was someone being bundled out of the room? There seemed to be a deliberate slowness in Cosmina's walk back to take her seat on the stage.

"AMAZING! Question from a member of the audience." Valentine didn't believe this. "What about football? What about the national game?"

"I am delighted to confirm that football won't be allowed in schools for children aged twelve and above, but there will be more opportunities for competitive football outside the school gates. I've been given special authority to announce a major expansion of community sports grants. We're not proposing removing the contact element from amateur football, at least not yet. We predict a big rise in solo mime inside schools to fill the gap."

"ABSOLUTELY AMAZING! OUR SCHOOLS ARE HURTLING TOWARDS AN UNBELIEVABLE FUTURE!"

Who could disagree? A pause followed: a chance for reflection. Spads sat back and beamed across the room, showing a talent for wearing a fixed smile longer than most. Cosmina reinforced the messaging, reading out the bullet points on the screen. She quickly switched to shouting, as some in the audience had begun to chat. Too many to throw out.

Valentine and Dinners put on their public-facing masks to prepare to mingle during the networking buffet. The thought of having to endorse this nonsense left Valentine feeling numb, and he ventured a bit of hushed honesty in Dinners' ear to reassure himself.

"He reckons, thinks, expects, predicts. Where's the research? Where's the evidence? Does it even exist?"

"Shut yer cake 'ole, Val," shot back the reply, putting Valentine back in his place.

11

The networking buffet felt interminable as the audience had lots of questions. Spads, Cosmina, Valentine and even Dinners were mobbed by guests, although Dinners was having none of it and batted away questions by getting stuck into the buffet and splattering anyone foolish enough to come near him. Cosmina was taking plenty of questions, but Spads was shamelessly allowing the junior advisers to monopolise his time. Valentine found himself mimicking Cosmina, mainly repeating the bullet points she had shouted out at the end of the presentation with a confident smile.

Once the last of the visitors had gone, Dinners suddenly switched from gluttonous vacancy to athletic haste. He gave Cosmina the most direct instruction she had ever received during her time in Whitehall, which took her so much by surprise she forgot to push back. She left to check the junior advisers could manage their game of danced office football unsupervised before joining them in five minutes. Next he ushered Spads and Valentine into a side room where they stood ignoring each other, each contemplating his next move. Dinners appeared to be in a hurry and, to Valentine's relief, Spads was the first target.

"Well done, son. Ah reckon linkin' owt t' fooball's a winner. Now sit down f' the bad news."

The mixed comment had a dramatic effect on a surprisingly-brittle Spads, who was only expecting more praise. He crumpled into a chair. Dinners lowered his volume and slowed his delivery.

"The PM didn't watch yer film.'e's too busy t' waste 'is time on 'alf-baked ideas, even good uns. Count y'self lucky 'e wasn't kept waitin'. If 'e 'ad the 'ole lot a ye would be swirlin' round t' plug 'ole 'bout now. 'ave ah got through to ye?"

Spads tried to speak, but there was no volume. After a bit of heavy kneading on Spads' fragile ego, Dinners got down to the business at hand.

"Don't worry, son. Ah'm the PM's eyes n' ears. Ah was stress testin' the 'ole thing, thinkin' the worst. Ah think Val 'eard a bit?"

Valentine nodded, safer than saying anything.

"An ah think there might be summat 'ere. Thank yer minister f' that. 'e asked the key question."

This was one of those moments when an office persona malfunctioned revealing a truth usually kept well hidden. Spads couldn't have expected his triumph would be followed by a grilling sanctioned by No.10 in front of the minister whose nominal seniority meant nothing in the wider game. When Dinners credited Valentine with the most important stress test for his greatest idea to date, Spads couldn't stop his disgust being plainly written on his face.

"Yer minister asked where's the evidence we can use the law t' stop young 'uns squabblin' an' scrappin' with each other at school? Where's the research be'ind yer film?"

Silence from Spads, because there was no research behind his latest schooling hack. Both he and Dinners knew this was the sort of radical thought experiment the government needed to maintain escape velocity from accountability. Dinners had even given Spads the contacts he needed to get the film produced to an impossible deadline. So, why belittle him in front of this out of favour minister? They both knew Front had marked Valentine's card. A wave of indignation swept through Spads, giving him the resolve to find his voice.

"The evidence is out there. We just need to find it."

Dinners laughed.

"Now yer gettin' it, son. Ah'm made up for ye. Decide what ye want first, 'ow t' sell it next, then 'ow t' get it last. The only way government gets owt done. If we can't find what we need, we'll tack on a nice made up case study. We're talkin' a proper bloody schoolin' revolution 'ere!"

The surprises continued. Cosmina knocked on the door and could be seen through the glass waiting patiently to be invited in. It added to the lustre Dinners was now casting across the room. Spads waved Cosmina in like he was in charge.

"We need to find a school to support the anti-bullying initiative. We can give them a range of scenarios to back up with school data."

But Dinners wasn't listening to Spads.

"Now, are ye ready f'r me good news? Me team's bin lookin' f'r a school t' cook up the case studies we need."

Cosmina pitched in. "Can't we get a real school to help us with the entire schooling revolution?"

"Like yer ambition, but that kind o' school don't exist. Let's stick t' sortin' out yer bullyin' brainwave."

Valentine felt like a bystander in all of this.

"I'll make the tea," he said as he slipped out of the room. No one seemed to notice.

12

As soon as he was outside of the room Valentine felt better, remembering he was the previous Home Secretary and was still really a Secretary of State. He walked in the direction of the office kitchen, but reality-checked his subservience to these special advisers, and swerved back to his own office. He reflected on how easy it was to feel normal after you left a stressful environment, and this helped him see Front's current hold over him as a temporary phase that would pass as all things do. He was suddenly feeling very rational, so decided to face some of his demons in the relative safety of his office. He worked up a concise list summarising the schooling revolution ahead, which he copied onto his office whiteboard.

Help every lesson – copy out that text
Help teachers with assessment – sign off that copying out
Help teenagers to behave – don't break the law

He hoped having this displayed in his office might prompt some reflection from Spads and Cosmina about the schooling cliff edge ahead. And if that didn't work, his deliberate mistake with the anti-bullying initiative must surely start a conversation?

Just as Valentine got comfortable daydreaming about a schooling change of direction …

"Mine's black, two sugars, ye lazy sod." Dinners burst in as Valentine didn't nearly fall off his chair.

The impromptu meeting with Dinners had a less than promising start, with Valentine scrambling back onto his chair and trying to get comfortable. Dinners had already noticed the whiteboard.

"What, a Cabinet minister oo knows nowt 'bout marketin'? Lucky f'r you we've just given this stuff the 'ard sell. Yer too serious by arf!"

But Dinners delivered this put down wearing a benevolent smile. He seemed comfortable walking on an event horizon.

"Ah need a confab with ye before ah leave, coz it's at a delicate stage. Ah'm late, so shut up an' listen. Ye can process later."

Valentine nodded.

"Way ah see it, schoolin's always got a kickin' as a political football. Change f'r change's sake; we've trained voters to expect it. Look what's 'appened t' schoolin' in me own lifetime. Grammar, then no grammar, then grammar's back. Rote learnin' an' dictation binned f'r creativity an' group work, then bairns know nowt, so 'ere's knowledge rediscovered 'iding in the cupboard. Killin' off exams looks like a risky move, ah'll grant ye, but we've bin yo-yoin' with easier an' 'arder exams f'r years. An' in most of me school visits; ah've seen bairns copyin' summat out.

"But 'e may be goin' too far with this punt t' sort out school bullyin'. 'e turned up at No.10 with some 'alf-baked schoolin' behaviour idea scribbl'd on a piece o' paper. Ye must know 'ow desperate 'e is t' stay in Front's good books? Well, ah suggested gettin' the law involved t' test 'im out. An' 'e bloody ran with it! Took it straight t' Front be'hind me back.

"It's me own bloody fault. Ah should 'ave realised grabbin' ev'ryone's attention comes first. Ah'm t' blame f'r this mess in the makin', Val, so ah've bin tryin' t' recover the situation. An ah' think ah've got a plan that could work. Ah think ah may 'ave found a school that can back up the punt an' the inevitable flip-floppin'. But ah need ye t' check it out f'r us. Ah need yer wider government experience, Val. Will ye do it? Ah need yer answer NOW!"

Valentine was taken aback by the apparent candour in Dinners' analysis. He'd welcome a holiday from his default paranoia, but he couldn't be sure what Dinners was up to. Was he in on Front's plans for his humiliation? Or was this surprising encounter something else entirely? Whatever the case, he was getting more reconciled by the day to premature retirement. He said yes to Dinners' request, perceiving there might be a shift in his situation ahead, and he was right.

The best school in the world

1

Front's grandiosity hit a new level of Cabinet meeting menaces. Poor "lazy" Strong. She started to present a "solution" to the perennial problem of police overtime. Valentine was sure private hire policing wasn't her idea. The hours of Home Office time it must have taken to calculate the regional ratios of potential gigs per officer. Unless it was just made up. That couldn't be ruled out. All the same, the Prime Minister's dabbling was all over it. Not changing police contracts generally, but making it opt in. Officers who opted in wearing a camouflage green police helmet, illustrated by a granite-faced bobby on the steps of No.10. Front rounded off the item himself, going through the motions. There were no objections or even questions because members of the Cabinet were cowed in awe or fear by the singular immaturity chairing the meeting. With one exception. Front cast a self-satisfied sneer across the table and ended proceedings abruptly, walking over to Valentine's chair.

"In there, NOW!"

Valentine was unfazed now he'd accepted the ride he was on, and dutifully followed the order. Dinners was already seated in the room Valentine stepped into. They acknowledged each other but said nothing, waiting for Front's tiresome need to make an entrance. Valentine decided to stand, keeping his hands in his pockets and shuffling some imaginary dirt on the floor to give off enough of a quizzical detachment to wind the Prime Minister up. The door slammed and Front showed what he was made of.

"You can sit down, you know?"

Valentine stayed standing, so Front sat down and quickly got agitated.

"Now listen, Vaklerner. Stop dwelling over ancient history and start showing a bit of real leadership for once. Look at what lazy Strong is achieving over at the Home Office, breaking new ground unheard of in your day."

Valentine agreed with this.

"You need to step up the same at Schools. You've got no excuses: the most thought-provoking set of advisers anywhere; more policy hacks to play with than any other ministry; and now my very own office has found you a way to make the biggest one happen. Let me make this absolutely clear: we shouldn't be doing your strategic work for you. This is your last chance, Vaklerner. Don't mess it up!"

But Valentine was serene. The pep talk with an under-performing minister routine wasn't pressurising him. They were all under-performing because of who controlled the game. He pressed the red button.

"If something's bothering you, Prime Minister, spit it out."

Dinners' towering frame suddenly stood up, taking Front's attention off losing it with Valentine. The power dynamic wobbled.

"Found a school for the bullying hack for Christmas."

"You mean the anti-bullying hack?"

"Shut up and listen! Dinners did some preliminary checks, but you're the minister, remember? Long day ahead. Clear your diary tomorrow. Six o'clock start."

"Clear my diary tomorrow for what long day?"

"You're leaving at six tomorrow morning."

"Hold on there, Pleasant. Isn't this initiative a bit too radical, even for this government?"

"Don't you understand anything? Voters want radical ideas. And this government gets lifestyle politics. I'd be more worried if MPs from the kitchens and bathrooms party were sitting opposite me in the Commons."

With these nuggets of wisdom, the Prime Minister pelted out of the room.

Dinners followed slowly, his eyes and mouth unified in the faintest Mona Lisa smile.

"Fight an' then flight. See now why 'e beat ye t' the top job, Val? See ye tomorro' mornin'. Six o'clock sharp."

2

Valentine was already waiting when Dinners pulled up at five to six in an anonymous lower range government car. He gave nothing away about their destination beyond, "not far if ah was a bloody bird, but the roads a' crap." They settled into an uneasy silence as Dinners negotiated their route out of London. Valentine wondered where he was being taken to and allowed himself the odd short nap, which became easier with the monotony of the motorway. Then he was jolted awake.

"Yer safer than ye think, Val. Front still thinks yer career positive f'r 'im."

Dinners then seemed to flick a switch, discarding his politic taciturnity and monosyllabic put downs. Yes Front craved the limelight, but he wasn't totally blinded by his addiction. He knew his populist cult drove down the calibre of the team cast in his shade. Front didn't like it, but he couldn't get rid of all of his main rivals straight away. He still needed seasoned competence like Valentine Vaklerner in the Cabinet. Despite the blind corners on the country lanes he was now negotiating, Dinners turned to meet Valentine in the eye.

"'e thinks 'e's a thinker coz 'is 'alf-baked ideas keep on comin'. 'e thinks 'e can make 'istory. An' 'e thinks Grant can 'elp 'im."

"The only way he'll make history is through the law of unintended consequences."

Dinners nodded. That was why Valentine needed to make the most of his move to Schools, a demotion yes, but also a chance to *finish this business off*. Dinners heavily stressed this point, setting off Valentine's internal dialogue again. He did have something in common with Front after all. They both pulled their evaluation of colleagues back to a balance sheet. He thought Dinners might be "career positive" for him, at least for now. Even if that changed, Dinners had already helped him exchange some of his workplace stress for curiosity about what was in store. Time to talk about their destination.

"Can we dispense with the cloak and dagger? What's the name of this school?"

Surprisingly, it turned out the school didn't have a formal name. It wasn't fee paying, didn't advertise and didn't even have a website. This school had to be hunted down. The negotiations it took to set up this visit! But Dinners did tell him to look up its headteacher, Valeria Scape, on his phone.

Valentine was surprised by the search results. Nothing that originated less than twenty years ago. The latest reference to

Valeria Scape was in an article criticising her warnings about computer bugs threatening the real start of the millennium in 2001, long after IT systems had been successfully patched. Not very auspicious. Dinners gave some context. It showed how successful she was in dropping off the radar. She'd planned this misstep, hoped her critics would pounce, and they didn't disappoint. Valeria retired as a headteacher soon afterwards, then nothing. She'd as good as put her detractors to sleep, erasing memories of her as a player on the schooling circuit. According to Dinners, she dropped out to concentrate on her next schooling project. How did he know this? A question for later because Valeria Scape's back story started to flow out of Dinners unprompted.

3

"She must be in 'er early eighties by now. An' she's seen it all, 'as an authenticity most of us can only dream of."

It turned out Valeria was a late developer. She had only really hit her stride in the later years of her formal career, having put in decades of trying to get the best for the children under her care on the shifting sands of schooling priorities. As a new headteacher at the start of the '90's, Valeria happened to live directly opposite a converted chapel in Camden that was the city pad of a features editor from a Sunday newspaper. Grateful for the local grittiness scattered around the early gentrification, they were always on the lookout for material that chimed with the changing times.

Valeria sensed political change in the air and decided to play, developing a talent for deftly moving between opposing positions, initially without censure. She was helped by the liberalism of her benefactor, committed to keeping their readership on the cutting edge of the new. Valeria initially set her stall against a new national schooling curriculum, which could only damage the fragile flower of learning through regimentation, then executed a U-turn because the need for quality control was greater as an accelerator to tackle then historic levels of inequality. She then spent a few years honing her commentary, focusing on the rabbit hole she saw schooling receding into when a potentially good idea morphed into micro measurement for its own sake, making children and teachers work hard but not smart.

By the late '90s Valeria was writing about the move into an age of significantly shorter attention spans, with policies and messaging to match. She was calling for learning appropriate to context following two plain-speaking rules: do what works and don't waste children and teachers' time.

"'ave a look f'r 'er last speech."

This was at an emergency summer schooling conference. Valeria was advocating throwing away over-prescriptive curricula that undermined the usefulness of schooling outcomes. A tide of worsening behaviour could be reversed when children saw authenticity creeping back into their schooling. She made herself the target of a cohort levering their careers with the schooling panaceas of the day, and was roundly condemned by the people that mattered on the schooling policy circuit.

"She played a blinder. Can ye see why she kept warnin' 'bout obsolete computer bugs? Made 'erself obsolete an' she went underground 'ere."

They'd arrived? What, at a disused airfield with a collapsed hanger and a few derelict buildings? It had been raining and the depressing scene was magnified by reflections from the puddles all around.

"Oo in their right mind would choose this dump?"

4

It was a depressingly desolate scene on this murky autumn morning. Abandoned military buildings in various states of dilapidation were separated by broken concrete and mud. Dinners led Valentine on a walk that was no less tortuous for its short distance. This place hadn't just been abandoned; it had been laid waste. Valentine had to walk face to the ground to keep his footing. They edged towards an anonymous row of vandalised huts.

"Wipe yer feet on that."

Dinners pointed to a metal grille, which they made the best use of as they could.

"Now, follow me closely."

They both walked along the narrow path between huts three and four, turned a corner to face a door blended into its surroundings by the all-pervasive graffiti.

"Might 'ave t' wait a bit."

Nearly ten minutes passed and nothing happened. Valentine read the door and walls to take his mind off being tired, wet and cold. The graffiti was mostly banal. But there were also bits of philosophy hidden in there. *Everything is a prison in the end.* He thought about his own journey and smiled to himself. There was a life after the political humiliation Front was planning for him. Then something he recognised: *know thyself.* And when he scanned a bit more, there was its fellow from the Delphic oracle: *nothing in excess.* It made him aware of the excessive damp cold that was starting to make him shiver.

Mercifully, he heard a click and the door opened. Dinners gestured to follow him, but ignored Valentine's questions. This was a DIY arrival. Valentine followed Dinners down a poorly lit windowless corridor, painted an institutional light green. Nothing to announce what was coming next, and the dim lighting didn't help with the slight downward gradient and the ninety degree turns at irregular intervals. The final corner came almost immediately after the penultimate one, and his eyes had to adjust to the lights issuing from the far end of a large room. When his eyes adjusted, Valentine could make out the parquet floor, wood panelled walls and four solid wood doors opposite.

"We wait over there."

Dinners pointed at a row of three chairs along the wall at the far end of the room. Valentine followed, but was losing patience.

"Why all this theatre? Who are these people?"

But Dinners was still ignoring him, even when they sat down. Dinners looked blankly ahead.

5

After a few minutes the door furthest away from them was opened by a short woman with grey hair combed down severely from a middle parting, and wearing what looked even from a distance like industrial-strength spectacles. Apart from her utilitarian charcoal grey suit, there were no signs of a corporate identity. Dinners stood up, as if to attention, and Valentine did the same. Dinners walked in the figure's direction, so Valentine followed. She gestured for Dinners to go through the opened door. Valentine presumed to follow, but found himself standing still, almost hypnotised. She said nothing, but pointed an admonishing finger at him. Valentine got the message. He sat back down and was relieved she was walking back towards the doorway she had appeared from. But she closed the door from the outside and walked to sit on one of the parallel set of chairs along the opposite wall. Valentine felt like he'd been placed under surveillance.

He took out his phone to distract himself from the sentry opposite. He counted the internet search results for Valeria Scape to pass some time. He felt a bit bolder, so he tried to take a surreptitious photo of his surroundings. He selected the camera, but it didn't respond. He selected other functions, and most of them worked. His phone seemed to have been selectively disabled. The realisation made him more self-conscious again.

Then something happened to release him from his trap. The second door away from him was opened by a young woman, also wearing a charcoal grey suit. She noticed Valentine for a split second, but didn't react and walked over to the sentry. Something was exchanged and she walked over to the door Dinners had used, waited a few seconds for the red light to turn green and disappeared through the doorway.

Then his attention was taken by activities finally suggesting a school. The third door opened and a group of about twenty sixth formers entered the room. They all wore charcoal grey boiler suits with colour matched training shoes. They acknowledged the sentry respectfully, but no one spoke. They divided into two groups and disappeared through the two doors nearer to Valentine.

Within seconds these doors opened again and a group of younger children entered. They lined up in single file in front of door three and waited in silence for the red light to turn green. When it did, each child nodded to the sentry as they reached the doorway.

Door two opened again and a group of children started setting up the room for what appeared to be an assembly. It reminded Valentine of his own schooling back in the mists of time: none of today's ubiquitous technology, just a wooden lectern and rows of wooden gym benches moved from the sides of the room for seating. A boy was placing printed sheets on the benches. Valentine was curious, and got the boy's attention. The boy intimated he could read a copy, but snatched it away before it reached his outstretched hand. This broke the nostalgic spell.

"Ms Scape is ready to meet you now, Mr Vaklerner. Knock three times, wait for the light to turn green, and make sure you close the door behind you."

Valentine jumped. He hadn't noticed the sentry approaching. Her eyes were hard to make out behind the intense magnification of her spectacles.

There was no question he was going to follow her instructions.

6

Valentine closed the heavy door behind him and found himself in a room broken up by a number of doors, with framed newspaper articles covering the wall space. The room contained two wooden pews either side of a coffee table arrayed with mid-morning refreshments. He counted six doors in total, which felt a bit oppressive in such a small windowless space. The only door without a combination lock was labelled *bathroom*. Three of the doors led to *decks*: *exam*, *project*, and *play*. The door he had entered through imperiously declared *please leave*, and he expected the *Head of the school* door to open at any moment. But when it didn't, he was grateful for the down time.

He found himself in a surprisingly good mood eating a late buffet breakfast and reading the walls. The articles were like the good news stories usually blazoned across school receptions, but the subject matter was hard core. Nano tech innovations in surgery, new generation nuclear fail safe design, advances in applied corporate environmental awareness, successful mediation of a sectarian conflict. All of the articles attributed unexpected breakthroughs to corporations or institutes. He was certainly getting more interested in this visit and, thanks to the refreshments, had no problem being a bit more patient.

When a door eventually opened, it wasn't the *Head of the school* door in front of him. Valentine jumped out of his seat, and turned to face a tall woman with tied back grey hair, wearing the expected suit.

"Welcome Minister, Valeria Scape. I didn't mean to keep you waiting. We're having to schedule quite a few in-year admission interviews lately. You'll get a chance to see one later. You've got a busy day ahead of you before hamming it up collects you at five."

"Sorry, I don't understand?"

"A nickname for Mr Hamble, Mr Vaklerner. We developed a shorthand surprisingly quickly negotiating this visit."

"He does ham things up a bit."

"And it can be annoying, but he does get things done. You're here after all. Can we begin?"

"Please call me Valentine Vaklerner. I assume Mr Hamble has briefed you about the schooling revolution we're in the process of launching? The Prime Minister has asked me personally to evaluate your school's potential as a case study for a radical change we're hoping to launch on Christmas Eve."

"Forgive me, Mr Vaklerner. I must make clear from the start that we're also evaluating you to see if we can work together. If you want us to supply the case studies you're asking for, I must insist on a warts and all picture about schooling out there to see if we can back engineer what you need. We need to account for all possible scenarios to make this work, and we need to know if we can really work together. I'm sure you've been told nothing I could say about you in the outside world would be given the slightest credence?"

Valentine's interest kept on growing. Here was an offer to explore his fears about schooling with a seasoned school leader, who had just offered him the perfect cover. He'd have liked to know more before proceeding on these terms, but this was no time for prevarication.

"OK. I've been allocated a team of somewhat reality-challenged special advisers at the Ministry for British Schools. The lead adviser is Spads Grant, credulous and cunning in equal measure. His vision is to turn schooling into little more than a national child minding service. It's been hard work trying to inject a bit of sanity into his plans."

"Thank you for starting off so candidly, Mr Vaklerner. To me, this lot look like the logical extension of what I could see on the horizon twenty years ago. And too much power too quickly can send some people back to the playground. Your prognosis is dire, so I think we may be able to help. One of the main reasons for setting up this school is do the seemingly impossible. I think we may be able to package key parts your schooling revolution appropriately."

"Forgive me, but why did you set up this place when you could have retired?"

Fortunately, like many who had risen to the top of her profession, Valeria Scape didn't need much prompting to start a monologue. This was all it took to set her off with a potted history of the school.

7

In her later years as a headteacher on the outside, Valeria became excised by the disproportionate amount of time and effort she was having to put into protecting her children and teachers from the worst of the new initiatives seeping out of the Ministry for British Schools. She had tried to communicate the benefits of a less centralised and tick boxy approach to schooling upwards, but the churn of new initiatives kept accelerating. However, she had stroke of luck when she met Miss Class, the teacher Valentine saw outside her office, through one of the collaboration forums she had signed up to. Scape and Class led a schooling standards squad for a while, touring the country honing key issues, and planning their escape to make a distinctive contribution to schooling.

They went under the radar to create a self-funded school for children with an aptitude for leadership in a crisis – children who weren't well served in the wider schooling universe. They felt their decision had been vindicated by the last twenty years, with crises in all areas sadly becoming the norm.

"Thank you, Ms Scape, but how can you share your unregulated school with the Secretary of State for British Schools?"

Valeria smiled.

"Your visit isn't even a calculated risk for this school, Mr Vaklerner. The controls we have in place to manage our graduates who go rogue are more than enough to take on the government."

Rogue. Valentine smiled back. He thought about the Prime Minister finding out about this school, having a temper tantrum when he realised it was outside of his control. Would he turn bitter and snappy because he missed out on being schooled here himself? Would he even have got in? He was certainly familiar with crises, but he caused most of them himself, and he usually got out of the current mess by stoking a bigger one.

Next Valeria outlined the core philosophy and structure of the school. They had two overarching rules: *do what works* and *don't waste anyone's time*. They had a more traditional section, the *exams deck*, where children spent up to half of their time studying for the outstanding qualifications they needed as the entry ticket to their chosen career pathway. Once they left, they had to submit a detailed report about their activities back to the school every quarter. Failure to report adequately triggered a monitoring process that resulted in a sliding scale of intervention to maintain the school's mission to benefit wider society.

"We have mutually beneficial arrangements with a network of boarding schools where our children sit their exams. They get to declare our outcomes as their own, and we keep our anonymity. We've got a waiting list of schools wanting to join because our children always deliver. It also helped us recruit one of our best graduates. You'll meet her later."

"So, how do you feel about replacing exams with the new curriculum standard?"

"Not concerned at all. We'll do international exams. No government would turn its back on that soft power."

"You're probably right. But how can you guarantee excellent exam results with only half the curriculum time?"

"I said *up to* half of the curriculum time, Mr Vaklerner. I've already told you: we do what works and we don't waste time. We've cherry-picked some of the best ideas to support our mission."

"Like what?"

"Like skipping or repeating years to let children on different timelines reach a challenging standard. We do use quite a lot of rote learning so children perform in their exams. It allows us to release curriculum time for more interesting pursuits. The children see this, and don't waste any of their exam prep so they can spend more time in a collaboration trench they run themselves."

"A what?"

"Actually, two interdisciplinary collaboration trenches that synthesise theoretical and vocational learning. We've had to dig deep for the geothermal energy we need in the collaboration trenches. They're the main reason we have to be tracked down. We've only got 344 places at this school. We'd be overwhelmed by the demand."

Valeria explained how the children themselves made all the rules in the collaboration trenches, including the criteria to peer assess success. The collaboration trenches rejected age seniority and only tolerated hierarchy based on merit to get the most out of collaboration. The children only accepted external guidance through gentle teacher facilitation, and chose to judge themselves on their practical output. She often found that children could do incredible things without having all the words to explain their interdisciplinary work. The children created their own evaluation framework, and both collaboration trenches independently rejected classification as the starting point for learning.

"Can you misclassify pure innovation anyway?"

There was a manufacturing collaboration trench integrating science, engineering and applied arts (including the ergonomics and aesthetics of design) and a networking collaboration trench combining computing, finance and political activism.

"Politics with a use it or lose it urgency. There's only so much I can tell you in a meeting. We don't attach much importance to messaging without delivery. You'll get a better idea when you visit both trenches later to see the children in action. They're committed to innovation, which you only get through doing. I think it helps them cope with the hothouse cramming for exams knowing they spend a lot of their time in an environment they create themselves."

"What's first on the tour?"

"We'll start soon, but before I can let you out there I need to make something else clear about our school. It's more like a boot camp than a holiday camp. It's about developing high level skills so our graduates can step in as effective leaders in their careers. Our children like taking on difficult challenges, and they are tough on each other, but we have systems for setting and monitoring effective boundaries, and the ultimate penalty is expulsion followed by a lifetime of monitoring. We've hardly ever had to go there because the children understand what they'd be giving up. They see the school in very simple practical terms. They call the exams deck *don't waste time,* and their collaboration trench is *do what works*. What would happen to school behaviour out there if children saw schooling being structured around them?

Society's not ready to face up to its need for us, Mr Vaklerner, but it benefits from us in more ways than it knows. That's why we agreed to No.10's request to help you out. Making the seemingly unworkable function is a challenge our children will relish."

Valentine was mentally tripping over the questions multiplying in his head. He'd have liked to share his wider concerns about the state of the government, but he may have said too much already.

Fortunately, Valeria changed the subject.

"Let me show you our corner shop."

8

Valeria opened the *project deck* door and Valentine found himself in a corridor with a slight incline. They passed a group of children returning to the school, walking in silent single file. When they reached a metal door at the end of the corridor, Valeria took a bunch of keys out of a pocket in the lining of her coat. She opened the door, they stepped though, she locked the door behind them and repeated the same with the second door, which was made of solid wood. Valentine found himself in a dingy room lit through the opaque glass door opposite.

"Let me show you our shop."

They stepped through and adjusted to the natural light. They were in a room framed on two sides by large shop windows half obscured by gingham curtains, as was the entrance. Opposite were two walls covered floor to ceiling with wooden drawers with locks, all open and empty. The only furniture was a battered old table and some wooden stools.

"I'm interviewing here in a few minutes. You'll observe through the spy hole there. Just enough time to explain some of the work the children have put into this place."

Valeria explained that the shop was an integrated project space for both collaboration trenches, giving them direct access to the outside world. The manufacturing collaboration trench designed the shop as a historical throw back. They also manufactured the stock. The networking collaboration trench liaised with the public.

"What stock? The shop looks empty to me."

"We award bespoke badges to our customers in return for the donations they make. They've become so prized, it's only safe to bring each badge up from the school when we're about to award it. We keep each badge in one of these lockable drawers, and usually pretend we've forgotten which one to maintain the drama of a good shopping experience."

"Sorry, I don't understand. Shops don't award prizes in return for donations. What's going on here?"

"What's *going on* here, Mr Vaklerner, is that our children are experimenting with ways to mitigate the excesses of consumer culture. All our children are obsessed by climate change, probably because they have the capacity to analyse the consequences of insufficient action in detail. They've come up with an experiment to channel aimless consumption to more productive ends. It's meant to look like an empty old shop to give it kudos with the cohort they're targeting: young, well off and addicted to shopping."

"I don't see what's in it for them."

"It's the exclusivity. It goes like this. You exist in a peer group where everyone is rich and terrified of running faster and faster to escape boredom. You receive a mysterious letter out of the blue inviting you to donate cash to "make a contribution"."

"Contribution to what?"

"You also get the chance to visit a tastefully dilapidated shop like the one you've noticed but never visited on your well-heeled high street. You jump at the chance to do something so unexpected."

"Forgive my scepticism, Ms Scape, but it does remind me of my special advisers making up the world as they want it to be, and the rest of us scrambling around to square the circle. That's the reason I'm here, remember?"

"A superficial view if I might say so, Mr Vaklerner. You're here to get the research findings you need to match the conclusions they've already reached. Our children are the opposite of that. They do very thorough research so they're swimming with the tide.

There are plenty of wealthy young people desperately looking for something new. We know this because everyone selected turns up at their appointed time. They donate handsomely, and feel lucky to get their badge about making a lot less landfill. It works because we make a big play of it being obligation free with no follow up. It's the sense of release they're grateful for, however temporary. We know it's working from the number of people approaching us to offer donations when the news filters through their social networks. We make people who approach us wait, and we turn down a few to maintain the demand."

"Is this how you're funding the school, Ms Scape?"

"Not at all, Mr Vaklerner. None of these donations fund our school. We've got much more stable sources of funding."

"So, where does the money go?"

"This is where the networking children have been putting a lot of their effort, how to reroute aimless consumption to more positive ends. They tried using a detailed set of criteria to distribute the money, but it became the usual unfit for purpose means testing bureaucracy. Some of the children worried about becoming ruthless petty bureaucrats in deciding who got the money, so they've been trying something simpler; using the concept of acting without choosing to give away donations to people they bump into in the street. They're finding this works much better."

"That makes no sense at all! It's defeating the object of redistribution not to test it's being done correctly!"

"To be blunt, Mr Vaklerner, I'd expect that sort of response from a Cabinet minister. If I might say so, too much that comes out of government is based on over-elaborate systems that ultimately undermine themselves. The children pretend they're doing a human geography survey, ask random people how they would make appropriate use of a windfall, and usually hand over the money straight away. Anyway, there's your overview of the integrated project we use this place for. I'd get back there and get comfortable. They'll be here in a minute."

9

"They're here!"

Valentine scrambled for cover, mindful to close the door carefully behind him and tentative about approaching his spy hole. He took a few seconds to get into place and found he had a good view of the scene, behind Valeria seated facing three stools she had positioned at an angle so he could get a good view of the visitors. They weren't even here yet! But a few seconds later the doorbell shuddered. A smartly dressed woman entered, followed by an uncomfortably suited man. He turned around to close the door behind them as she stood surveying the scene. Where was their child?

Olive introduced herself and her husband Theo. Valeria reciprocated with Val Scape, and gestured for them to sit. Theo slumped onto a stool, shoulders down and arms folded, wearing a blank gaze. Olive gave Theo a cursory inspection, and then moved her stool closer to Valeria.

"I understand you want us to consider offering your son Oliver a place at our school. Will Oliver be joining us today?"

Valentine thought this was a bit passive, and so did Olive. She took charge, giving some context about her husband, a sporting scientific, and herself, a schooling consulter with a contact at the Ministry for British Schools – hence their visit here today.

"I'm afraid Oliver's too busy to join us today, but I can tell you everything you need to know."

"Thank you, very helpful. Please see today as a conversation where you have the opportunity to explain what Oliver can offer to our school. Can you persuade me to offer him a place?"

"Fair enough, but I'll also want a clear picture of what your school can offer him. He's a musician, a designer, a linguist and a debating champion, all at only thirteen: top grades across the board obviously …"

"Extra-curricular activities coming out of his ears?" Valentine didn't expect this from Valeria.

"Exactly. He couldn't be here today because he's got a French test he couldn't miss. He's promised me full marks."

"Thank you, I'm getting a much clearer picture. Could I unpick that last comment? What strategies would you say help Oliver feel confident about getting a perfect score in his test today?"

"That's easy. He puts in the time because he wants to make us proud."

"Could I have a second strategy?"

"I've given you two strategies."

"Oh, I see, very helpful. What does Oliver do to relax in his free time?"

"He likes team spo...." Theo suddenly realised his mistake.

"He's taken up Latin."

"He must be firing on all cylinders most of the time?"

"Yes, his work ethic is slowly getting there."

"Anything you want to add, Theo?"

"We speak with one voice, Ms Scape. Let's make sure we understand each other. Everything we've achieved with Oliver is being threatened by the schooling reforms we know are in the pipeline. No practical learning. What will studying French be like this time next year?"

"Advanced colour in the croissant?" Valeria's flippancy wasn't appreciated by Olive, who now looked like thunder.

"Let's not digress. I'm getting a much better understanding from our discussion, but it would help if we could focus on what Oliver could bring to the school. We *are* committed to practical learning here, but it's a tough environment. Children at this school need to be resilient because there's nothing like the pastoral care you might be used to."

"That's not a problem, Ms Scape. Oliver's pretty tough already, and I know this because he's sworn an oath to meet every one of my expectations."

"Thank you. Of course, the second strategy you mentioned earlier. It's all coming into focus now. Can I ask one further question?"

"Please go ahead, now we're on the same page."

"What practical skills can Oliver bring to our school?"

Olive was suddenly lost in thought. Theo's taciturn haunch stirred with an idea which remained unsaid thanks to Olive's withering stare.

"So many examples, Ms Scape, it's hard to choose."

"Just one example will do. I'm afraid our time's nearly up."

A disgruntled Olive looked like she was being forced to brainstorm with time running out at the end of an exam. She offered Oliver's achievements as a designer. When Valeria sketched the remit of the manufacturing collaboration trench, Olive swelled with pride at the wisdom of her choice, but she wasn't on top of the detail. Oliver spent last summer shadowing at a design museum. A type of internship. His many product designs.

"No, can't think of any specific examples. His achievements? Yes, more like his potential. You're right, more like my … HIS ambitions."

"Thank you so much for attending Oliver's interview today. I've got a much clearer picture of his application. We're getting a lot of mid-year admission applications lately, and people are waiting up to six weeks to find out if their child has got to the next stage, a day at the school. But I do have some good news for you. I don't think you'll have to wait that long for a decision."

"Thank you, Ms Scape. If we could hear from you by the end of this month, I can make sure we include your school with the other offers we're expecting by then."

"No, a final thank you to both of you. Even in Oliver's absence you may have helped us fast track the process."

Olive had heard what she wanted to hear and their departure was abrupt.

Through his spy hole Valentine saw Valeria walking slowly towards the outer door. Once the door was locked he emerged from his lair, and saw Valeria looking pensive.

"What chance Oliver can get to the next stage?"

"None at all."

"How could they think of not bringing Oliver to his own interview?"

"That's not the ultimate reason. I'm deciding how to manage the message and, more importantly, manage Olive. We can walk and talk."

10

Once they were descending into the bowels of the building, Valeria started to share her thinking.

"Most of our successful admission interviews involve a parent or guardian trying to find a mechanism to help develop a child's exceptional potential. They don't need to have achieved anything and, more often than not, over achievement means we've got more work to do. My alarm bells start ringing when I see a child over achieving mainly to please their parent. Where parental validation depends on what a child does rather than who they are. I can almost see Oliver's anxiety; feeling like someone else's project. It can become very brittle, and there's sometimes a reckoning one day. There's a higher chance of mental breakdown later in life. And do you know why?"

"Overload. Everyone has a saturation point."

"Yes, but that's the obvious answer. It seems counter-intuitive, but sometimes a breakdown can be a choice, to experience something primal and real in a life of conditional validation. Our personal pilot lights can be nurtured, Mr Vaklerner, but they must be triggered from within. But I'm digressing. My priority has to be managing Olive."

"She's not going to take no for an answer, is she? She might think you've taken one of her oaths."

Valeria ignored the attempt at humour.

"I've got two main options. We could contact her sooner saying the decision might take longer because of the volume of applicants, and we totally understand if she's already accepted another offer by then and we miss our chance of admit Oliver. We'd ask her to keep in touch with updates about Oliver's achievements."

"Have you thought of going through Theo?"

"That's clearly a nuclear option. And if there are other offers, I'm sure Olive will be straight back in touch to play us off against each other. I'm going to meet her deadline, and I'm going to play it like we can't offer Oliver anything like the level of curriculum challenge he needs to meet his potential. I'll thank her for helping us trigger a much needed review of standards at the school."

"That's a risk."

"Of course it is. We all dance on an event horizon here, Mr Vaklerner. I remember when we interviewed Dinners, as you call him. That was a real poker game."

"Dinners attended this school?"

"Keep up, Mr Vaklerner. We appointed him as a teacher."

"What did he teach?"

"Geography, politics and healthy eating."

"An unusual combination."

"Not if you want healthy and confident young people able to find their way in the world. We only employ polymaths here, Mr Vaklerner. He only left us to practise his own activism in a suitable setting. He was the first teacher we appointed after a lot of false starts. He made an instant impression at interview. He walked into my office handing me a contract I'd apparently signed to repurpose the site as a retail park. The bulldozers were already on the perimeter, scheduled to start the demolition in thirty minutes. And what impressed us was he waited another twenty-nine minutes to show us the exit clause. I think my indifference to the whole thing showed him he could refine his teaching craft here."

Valentine had found the familiarity between Valeria and Dinners a bit suspect, but he had to repeat this revelation to himself to believe it. The Prime Minister's special adviser appeared to be an operative of some sort on a mission. Everything pointed to Valentine being let deeper and deeper into a confidence.

"Hebden Hamble became Dinners, hiding in plain sight in the Westminster village and goading all comers to call him out as an imposter. But no one has. The whole thing is totally ludicrous, but he carries it off because of his confidence and, no offence, because of the low calibre of professional politicians and their hangers-on. Hebden credits his detour from healthy eating as the key ingredient that's maintained the theatre of it all for the last seven years. You are only here today, Mr Vaklerner, because Hebden has succeeded in weaving himself into the Whitehall machine."

11

Valentine had returned to the anteroom outside Valeria's office, enjoying a very good buffet lunch while she caught up on business. For a short time he sat opposite two children, a girl and a boy who had arrived with another boy who had disappeared into Valeria's office with a slight swagger. There was no acknowledgement of the visitor by either of them, nor did they occupy themselves as a displacement. They stood up when Valeria's door opened, and waited to walk behind her crestfallen visitor, who gave off an air of having been processed. Valeria appeared at the door and gestured for Valentine to stay seated. She sat opposite and fixed him with an intense stare.

"Before we visit the collaboration trenches, Mr Vaklerner, I need to make sure you understand a few more things. These areas are the children's domain. They set the rules and judge the outcomes. They can get quite trenchant with each other to get the most out of collaboration. Teachers only make suggestions. The children develop such a shorthand with each other; you may not even notice all of the interactions taking place in front of you. That's why rule number one is *don't ask questions until you are explicitly invited to do so*. I don't want to worry you but, if you break their flow, I may have to get you out of there quickly. The second rule is just as simple and very easy to follow: *stick to the path* you'll see clearly when we're in there. Don't think about venturing off it unless invited to do so, if you want to be certain of getting out without incident. All clear?"

Because his throat felt dry, Valentine nodded.

Valeria clapped enthusiastically as she stood up. "Let's go, then. We've got lots to show you."

12

They returned to the room where he and Dinners had arrived, which now looked more like a school assembly hall. Valeria knocked on the door closest to where Valentine had sat under Miss Class's unsettling gaze, and seconds tipped into minutes as they waited for the red light to turn green. Even the headteacher was being kept waiting and, to pass some time, Valentine examined the stage set now framing the wooden lectern, a mix of cityscape and rolling countryside below the sun's rays emerging from behind the clouds. He was fascinated by the intricate level of detail he hadn't expected in something so thin.

"Are we ready to go in, Mr Vaklerner?"

Valentine scurried over to the open doorway, and entered the manufacturing collaboration trench feeling a lot less composed than he would have liked.

He was in a short corridor that gave way to a large open space that looked like a factory production line. Valeria was already in the open space a few metres ahead of him. She was gesturing, pointing at him, then down at the floor. Check: he looked down and saw the path he needed to stay on, a different shade of grey and not very wide. Thumbs up to Valeria, and he walked towards her. She didn't speak but furiously pointed at him again, and he stopped, confused, until he realised he hadn't closed the door behind him. He had to turn around carefully to stay on the path while retracing his steps. When he caught up with Valeria, Valentine was starting to feel the expectations of the place weighing down on him.

Valentine could see groups of children working calmly together in hushed tones. They were wearing the smart boiler suits he'd seen earlier. The machinery around them varied in size and shape: a lot of it looked like 3D printers, and on an impressive scale. The scene was quiet for a factory floor, with a gentle humming background noise. Valeria appeared to be surveying the scene herself. They were both waiting, and he was following the two rules, so he ventured a question.

"So this is the science, engineering and design section? Can you explain to me how the different elements fit together in here?"

Valeria snapped back. "No, I can't! This isn't another school cross curricular project. This is genuine, integrated interdisciplinary work. I've already told you the children run things in here: it's about doing, not talking."

Valentine kept the decibels low and snapped back himself. "So, while we're both waiting to be spoken to, can you at least tell me what's happening in front of us?"

"You'll just have to wait until some of the children are ready to explain. Can you manage that, Mr Vaklerner?"

They both now stood in silence, waiting to be spoken to. Some of what was happening in front of them became a bit clearer. A group of children appeared to be maintaining one of the larger machines. While Valentine was finding the waiting a bit wearing, he was impressed at how deeply absorbed the children were in their work. It all seemed very different from copying out the cracking new schooling curriculum that Spads and Cosmina kept boasting about. He did know a bit of schooling jargon, and wondered if he was looking at the best kinaesthetic learning through doing that could be part of the solution to the schooling mess the country was in. But he also knew it was out of favour as an expensive strategy that couldn't be implemented effectively without empowering teachers.

How did the school pay for all of this?

13

Then a group of children left the machine they were working on to stand at the edge of the path in three neat rows. A boy in the front row spoke first.

"What you can see is stage 1 of our latest consumption experiment. The machines are working around the clock to test our hypothesis that cheap on-demand shopping produces a frenzied consumer peak that plateaus and eventually tails off. No sign of shopper fatigue in the test group yet, but some are down to five orders per day."

"Those machines look like 3D printers. What are you using them for?"

A girl left the front row and whispered something in Valeria's ear. She nodded in agreement.

"You've broken the first rule, Mr Vaklerner, but you're in luck. Any more rule breaking and we're both out. Understand?"

"Wait to be invited to ask questions and stay on the path," Valentine whispered back sarcastically. He didn't like being sarcastic, but he was feeling patronised. The children must have heard him because a girl in the middle row continued the explanation.

"We recruited a group of compulsive shoppers. We let them order as many products as they want from our catalogue. Every product costs one pound, and we don't charge for postage and packing. We don't let them show off to their friends. If they do, they get dropped. Do you have some questions for us?"

Valentine looked at Valeria. She nodded.

"You said stage 1. What is stage 2 of your experiment?"

"Stage 1 is shopping saturation and stage 2 is sustainable consumerism in its place. If we can cure a shopping addict, we want to help them value quality products and make less waste."

"Don't people want more expensive items?"

A boy in the front row chipped in. "We have a special formula. We 3D print compostable moulds in any shape. Add water and our special granules. Sets solid in ninety seconds. You can have a plate, a chair, a table, and lots more all for the same price. The moulds and granules all fit in the same small parcel. Let us show you."

Two of the children broke away and fetched what looked like a large plastic bag. Another child fetched a hosepipe and started to fill the bag with water. When an armchair took shape the hosepipe was removed: a pinch of something was dropped into the opening, which was held tightly shut. Another child gave updates from their stopwatch. "Thirty seconds," and the viscous vibration stopped. "One minute," prompted the child to let go of the opening: the armchair securely held its shape. "Time's up," and the group ripped off the biodegradable coating to reveal a red armchair that wouldn't look out of place in a Christmas shop window display.

"Would you like to try it out?"

Valeria raised her hand to gesture this was OK. The armchair easily supported Valentine's weight. All it needed was a cushion.

"Try to pick it up," which he did easily. The material was fibrous and strong, but incredibly light.

"Now stand back."

Another child poured a few drops from a test tube onto the armchair, which started to fizz and liquefy. The child carrying the hosepipe started to rinse the residue down a drain. Valeria coughed, and Valentine realised he was expected back on the path. The moment he complied the commentary resumed.

"Like the moulds, our products are plant based and dissolve into an organic residue. Our consumers love it: no hoarding or fly tipping needed. We take away the barriers to let them keep shopping as fast as they want to, everything at the same low price. Our best chemists created the formula, our engineer specialists built the fastest 3D printers, and our applied artists recruit and manage the consumer cohort, but we're all able to oversee any part of the project."

"You're a research school like the best universities."

The children instantly reverted back to their previous tasks. Valentine's compliment had been taken as a second unprompted question.

"Time to leave, Mr Vaklerner."

Valeria nudged him back to the entrance. She only spoke once the outer door was securely closed behind them.

"I hope you've got a sense of how the collaboration trenches work, Mr Vaklerner? It's all about results and not, dare I say it, messaging."

"Have you thought about patenting the formula?"

"Is it me, Mr Vaklerner, or do you keep bringing things back to money?"

"You could be missing out on the eco market."

"It's not as simple as that. Scaling up the 3D printing to mass market levels could create problems. The children's original aim was to find a class of physical assets as environmentally friendly as the digital assets we're developing. They've concluded that isn't possible, and their new aim is steer people into taking care of quality products, making less waste overall. What we saw is a ring-fenced project to understand how to wean people away from excessive consumption. We've only made one little foray outside the project, sent Hebden a chair that got him out of a tight spot with Percy Klepthappy."

"Who?"

"I thought you were a member of the government, Mr Vaklerner? Percy Klepthappy's the Prime Minister's new sycophant-in-chief. You'll soon know it if he becomes his new chief special adviser. Hebden has had a good run, but everyone gets cycled out eventually. Klepthappy's cabal tried to ambush him in a meeting last week. Luckily, Hebden sat him on our chair, added a few drops of our special solution, and before he knew what was happening Klepthappy was sitting in a puddle on the floor. Everyone was laughing so much they forgot why they were there. It's bought us some time. And talking of time, time we visited the networking collaboration trench."

14

The networking collaboration trench for computing, finance and political activism had similarities to the manufacturing section, but a different vibe. The children all looked engrossed in their activities, wearing boiler suits with the tailored lapels. From his clearly-marked path Valentine could see two valleys that were forested at the back, with stepped seating emerging from the foliage. Both were divided into zones for individual and group work. To his right was a wall, almost within touching distance, embedded with banks of computer servers. A stark difference in this section was the animation in the children's interactions.

"Debate is a staple in this here," Valeria added. She appeared more at home than before, and started the explanation herself when they reached the first group.

"This group are looking at organisational dysfunction. It's part of a bigger piece of work trying to align professed organisational values with the reality on the ground. They set up a control simulation with a cabal who run things in their own interests and pass accountability down the line. The other half set up a similar cabal, but with push back upwards to make the top accountable and flatten the overall structure. The performance management cycles are all speeded up, a yearly cycle takes a month, and they're over a decade into the simulation."

Valentine thought about Whitehall, but kept this to himself. "What are they finding?"

"No surprises. The control simulation has a well-oiled blame culture with a rapid staff turnover, and when it gets really bad an occasional Shakespearean cull at the top to reset the hierarchy. The other simulation is working through a middle management revolt. The middle refused to pass the rubbish on their plates down to their subordinates. They all failed their performance management, and they set up a virtual forum so they couldn't be atomised and picked off. It produced a crisis at the top, a lot of "we are where we are" pronouncements eventually leading to a more equitable in sharing out targets ... only when the bullying failed, mind you. They're using the experiment to develop a template to force hierarchical organisational structures to flatten. This group all report very high satisfaction with their work: they're working through scenarios they can use to troubleshoot in their careers."

"How long before someone speaks to us?"

"Impossible to say. They're not much inclined to give up a good argument to speak to visitors. That's why I'm filling in some of the gaps. I hope you can see by now that the collaboration trenches give our children hands-on experience of innovation for their careers? Someone has to lead on improving productivity in this country. Let's move on."

In the next valley most of the children were gathered around large monitors.

"Let *me* talk finances now, Mr Vaklerner. You've been speculating about how we fund this school. Well, what we've got here hasn't gone live yet, buts it's an option for balancing the budget in the future. This group are developing a new digital asset class and potential currency. The plan is for us to retain a significant majority of the limited issue, invite in institutional investors on Miss Class's books, and sell off small amounts of our original stake when the price reaches new peaks."

"What are Miss Class's books?"

"Her contacts on the outside: she's from a business and economics background. Our modelling suggests we can get twenty-nine years of funding out of it before it all crashes."

"Isn't this a risky bet to pin the school's future on?"

"We've got an advantage, Mr Vaklerner, but if I tell you you'll have to stay here with us."

Valentine couldn't tell whether Valeria was being serious or not. He turned to face the wall, taking in three distinct areas of computer server. He looked right and saw the lightly humming bank of computers opposite the first valley they had visited. He looked left and saw even more frenetic activity. But the computers in front of him didn't even look switched on. He evaded Valeria's question.

"What's in the next section? The computers look like they're on overdrive."

"You haven't answered my question, Mr Vaklerner. Do you want to know why our digital asset class has the edge?"

Valentine turned around slowly to look Valeria in the eye.

"Only if I can leave in one piece, Ms Scape."

Valeria smiled.

"You won't be surprised that it comes back to climate change, Mr Vaklerner. The children won't tolerate unsustainable energy usage for our digital assets. I'll let Persephone tell you about the quantum computing we're experimenting with. You wouldn't think she's only twelve."

15

Valentine was slightly taken aback when a young woman approached them, smiling and extending her hand.

"Let me introduce Iphigenia Plant. She's taking the work Hebden started with our children to new heights."

"Pleased to meet you, Mr Vaklerner. So, you're the latest captain of schooling policy?"

Valentine ignored the sarcastic delivery.

"Yes, I'm here to see if we can work together on a new project."

"I'm aware of that, Mr Vaklerner. I did my own work on a government schooling project. But what interests me is your relationship to your ministry. I'm assuming there must be a critical tension for you to be invited here to visit us?"

Valentine didn't want to give a Whitehall response, so just smiled back.

"Don't you recognise me, minister? You must have been around in Westminster when I had my moment with the Ministry for British Schools?"

Now her tone was ironic, bordering on patronising. He'd had a vague sense of recognition from the moment they met. Then it hit him. *More revision please.*

"The exams tragedy. Are you Iphigenia?"

"Yes, I was front of house at the schooling policy circus a few years ago, but I refused to stick to the script. Is the same old dabbling still limping on?"

Valentine couldn't take on Iphigenia's challenge.

"Relax, minister; you wouldn't be here if Hebden hadn't vetted you. And don't worry; I know all about the latest schooling standards squad, low standards so everyone "succeeds"."

Iphigenia ostentatiously traced quotation marks in the air to reinforce how unimpressed she was.

"I know you're in deeper than I was, but there's always a way out. I was as weary with that revision drill as you look now, but my agent got me out and I ended up doing my exams boarding with two girls from this school. I got them to say more than they were supposed to, but my real stroke of luck was they reported each other back to the school. Hebden was pulled out of Westminster to close down the situation. He ended up offering me a place in the sixth form here, and I came back after university to teach. Surely I've said enough to get you to lighten up, minister?"

"I'm told you've cracked quantum computing to mine digital assets on negligible energy use?"

"That's right, but the credit has to go to one of our youngest recruits. Persephone also runs an inset day we've been selling to the big tech companies to help them engineer AI with the necessary safeguards to maintain a sustainable equilibrium with humanity. She'll be along in a minute."

"What makes this Persephone so special?"

"Hard to put it into words but, put it this way, she's got three supercomputers running scared. You wouldn't think she only arrived last year. She's got a very rare skill. Miss Class has it too. You'll get the idea when you see her assembly later. Here's Persephone now. DO WHAT SHE SAYS!"

Iphigenia's expression matched the sudden tension in her voice. Valeria added a nod to take this seriously.

Valentine noticed a small girl emerging from the forest at the back, walking slowly in their direction. Persephone struck an incongruous figure. She looked no older than twelve, but was dressed like an elderly Margaret Rutherford in a tweed suit, garnished with a pince-nez. Spads' fake monocle flashed across Valentine's brain and unsettled him. This was no time for humour; this was serious. He'd barely got used to not speaking until he was spoken to, but now he had to follow this child's instructions without question.

Persephone had no time for niceties.

"So, you're Valentine Vaklerner? Looks like we're going to have to do all the hard work to get you out of the mess you're in."

Valentine knew not to respond. Iphigenia and Valeria looked relieved. Persephone issued some instructions.

"Send us one of your hopeless schooling policy-makers. Someone we can have a proper fight with, and knock into shape. Don't take this personally, but someone who might be up to the job. Now GET OUT, and take her with you!"

There was one more area ahead, but Valeria nudged Valentine it was time for them to leave. They made quick goodbyes to Iphigenia, who walked away in conversation with Persephone.

"What happened there?"

"I'm so thankful Iphigenia has the skills to guide her. I hope you're getting a deeper understanding of why we set up this school, Mr Vaklerner? Think about what we're doing here, giving children a vent for their very particular talents. Isn't that what all schools are meant to do?"

As the person responsible for implementing schooling policy above ground, Valentine didn't know what to say.

"I hope you understand why we let children frame their own applied learning? We don't impose our own limits on them, like your schooling advisers looking to tick another box and move on."

Valentine smiled.

"Something else you should know about Persephone: she's slowly improving. She's aware of her intolerance now, although she could still go rogue. But the good news for you, Mr Vaklerner, is that she's on your side."

"Is she really on anyone's side?"

"She's interested in your schooling revolution and she can deliver, so the question is what do you want from us? You've only got Miss Class's assembly left, Mr Vaklerner, and then you've got a big choice to make."

16

Valeria was back in her office catching up on business. She shouted through the open door to the room where Valentine was processing.

"We've only got a short time after the assembly, Mr Vaklerner, so please feel free to shout questions through."

"Persephone expelled us before we saw the last valley. What was in there?"

"Our data dashboard. I get a feed of the main metrics and emergencies requiring action."

"What are the main metrics?"

"Mainly confidential, I'm afraid, but I can give you a hint. I mentioned our graduate surveillance where we've got concerns. We've got ways of, let's say, managing potential problems. Get the idea?"

"I think I do. I hope I'm not going to be tagged before I leave here today?"

"How do you know you're not tagged already?"

Fair comment, Valentine thought. Dinners could have switched him on already.

"Is there anything else you want to know about the current Ministry for British Schools?"

"Next question, Mr Vaklerner?"

"Tell me about Miss Class. What's her first name?"

"No one knows."

According to Valeria, Miss Class was the embodiment of teaching as a vocation.

"She says she's married to the job, but I always feel there's a paradox in that. While there's usually a nurturing aspect to the best teaching, it's a profession first and foremost. Teachers' goodwill has to be taken seriously, otherwise you encourage a toxic work to rule mentality that's hard to eradicate. In my experience, even in the so-called good times with the money sloshing around, if you've only paid lip service to teachers' work-life balance there'll be a small minority somewhere incubating discontent. My point is I never ever take our teachers' commitment to our children for granted. But I digress…"

Miss Class was originally a business and economics teacher in a sixth form who had dabbled in kinaesthetic learning long before it became fashionable, encouraging her students to shadow and then trade in the deregulated stock market. Her breakthrough came during a stock market correction, when she honed her skill in making more out of bear markets.

In his own way Valentine concurred. He was finding his career yielding more interest on the way down than it ever did on the way up.

"Look, there's something I need to deal with. Can you make your own way to the assembly? Time to see Miss Class in action."

17

Valentine entered the hall where he was only adult in front of rows of children sitting on gym benches stretching into the distance. The sound of his footsteps on the wooden floor made him self-conscious as he walked over to the single empty seat near the lectern, which he thought it wise to occupy. But the children weren't paying him much attention. They were all staring avidly at the lectern, waiting for Miss. She soon obliged, entering from the door to the *don't waste time* exams area, and opening the proceedings with a resonant clap between cupped hands.

"Thank you, children. The waiting is nearly over for this month's team prize. Thank you for all of the entries: you made it difficult for Ms Scape and I to pick the winners from such a strong field. All of the entries show how we can achieve more by collaborating together, but we think the winners show best how teamwork can innovate to change the narrative itself. And today our lucky winners will be recognised in front of an illustrious visitor, Valentine Vaklerner. He is the government minister in charge of all the schools in this country…. except ours, of course. Today our winners can show him why we might not only be the best school in the country, but the best school in the world!"

Miss Class turned to Valentine, handing him three envelopes and skipping introductions.

"Three winners, Mr Vaklerner. Hand an envelope to the member of each team who comes to the front."

The envelopes were identical. Valentine was about to ask …

"First we have this month's square medal-winning team. Congratulations to the team from manufacturing who have developed DNA keys for secure storage of our new digital asset class offline. Lina, please collect your team's prize."

As an older girl was making her way to the front, Valentine was trying to work out which envelope to present to her. Miss was ignoring his glances for guidance. But he needn't have worried. Lina took all three envelopes, examined their sealed contents, returned two envelopes, and walked back to her place.

"The triangle medal for this month goes to Evander's team from manufacturing for their range of waste-free dreaming products for dreamed homes."

Valentine jumped as Evander snatched an envelope out of his hand. He wasn't sure which one.

"But we might all have good reason to thank this month's circle medal-winning team. From networking, for the first non-tactical tantrum by artificial intelligence, Dan, please collect your team's prize."

"I'm telling you for the last time, it's Dam, for Damocles!"

Damocles ripped open the envelope as soon as he snatched it out of Valentine's hand.

"Fifteen collaboration minutes unmonitored? Is that it?" Damocles threw the envelope's contents onto the floor and walked off in disgust.

"A simple enough task, Mr Vaklerner," Miss exhaled in little more than a whisper. Then with another resonant clap she moved the assembly on.

"Now, does someone want to own up to something? You know it gets more serious if I have to tell you there's a problem."

Miss's softly-spoken question had an unsettling undertone. The atmosphere in the hall quickly changed. Valentine looked up and saw Miss fixing the audience with the oddest stare. It unnerved him and he looked the other way, scanning the audience. The children were giving nothing away, but Miss wasn't moving on.

"Your time's running out, children. 10, 9, 8, 7, 6, 5, 4, 3 ..."

A boy a few rows from the back stood up and addressed the hall.

"I tried to manipulate the shoppers I manage to be the first to hit the wall our models tell us to expect. I nudged my shoppers to buy more and more, faster and faster. Someone made me see my actions were risking the whole experiment, and I've started to clean up the data I corrupted."

"What do you think, children?"

"We might need to start the whole consumption experiment again. He didn't bring himself back in. He had to be persuaded. He should be expelled and tagged for life."

"Kim has given us a harsh starting position, children. Anybody want to mitigate the judgement?"

"I wouldn't trust him to wash his own data. Close down his access. Get someone else to clean it up."

"Thank you, Dorothy. It's looking serious for poor Polycrates. Anybody want to speak up for him before I decide?"

No one intervened. Polycrates was only the second child Valentine had seen at the school without a quietly assured confidence. Miss delivered her judgement.

"Removed from manufacturing pending completion of data analysis. Suspend the customer-facing side of the consumption experiment until we can fully assess the damage. Full time exam studies for Polycrates until we can take a final view."

Valentine thought the wait and see approach was reasonable, but Polycrates was angry.

"I don't come to school to spend all my time getting drilled for exams," he shouted as two children led him away.

"Anybody else want to own up to something, children? You know I read all your blogs and peer feedback before this assembly."

A girl near the front stood up, looking worried.

"I contacted the CEO of a hedged fund. I told her about our experiment to flatten hierarchies and improve accountability. She offered to buy our strategy for a nine figure sum to archive it."

"What?"

Miss didn't shout, but her incredulous tone triggered a reaction across the audience, as if carried by the wind.

"Do you know what you might have done? Clearly not, because you wouldn't have done it. Do you want to graduate into a world full of dysfunctional organisations that can't manage the hard choices ahead? I thought every child in this school prioritised protecting the planet for their own survival?"

The audience stirred in anticipation.

"What have you got to say for yourself, Eclipse?"

"I didn't share anything, honestl…"

"That's enough of that. Sit down."

Eclipse sat down, looking contrite. Some in the audience started to exchange whispers, and Valentine expected a feast of draconian suggestions from her peers. But Miss's response was unexpected.

"Never mind. No harm done. Don't do that again, Eclipse."

Someone in the audience muttered something.

"What was that, children? Could you speak up a bit?"

"That's not fair."

Miss left the lectern to stand directly in front of the audience.

"Life's not fair, children. I hoped we were teaching you to understand that. Assembly over."

"Exclude her to the exams deck."

"I think Eclipse has learned her lesson, children. Let's get back to our learning, shall we? Assembly over."

"Walk her out of school. Now!"

"ASSEMBLY OVER … CHILDREN!"

Trying to shout the rebellious audience into compliance looked like a bad move. Valentine felt a pang of pity for this much vaunted teacher dying on stage in front of him. Miss was doing nothing to calm the discontent. If anything, she was making it worse by just standing there, looking down at the spectacles she was wiping with a handkerchief. She looked up for a moment, speaking in a hushed tone.

"I – said – assembly – over."

The audience's anger suddenly flipped into a stunned silence, and an orderly silent dispersal began. Miss put her spectacles back on and turned around.

"I hope you found that useful, Mr Vaklerner. I'll take you back to Ms Scape's office for your final assessment."

18

Valeria had rearranged her office. Armchairs one side of a coffee table, an uncomfortable office chair for Valentine opposite.

"Now, Mr Vaklerner, do you have any more questions for us?"

"What happens on the play deck?"

"That's our online gaming area. Think about what we saw in the collaboration trenches, Mr Vaklerner. To make collaboration sustainable our children need to know the limits of interaction. They learn this through regular gaming sessions on the play deck. This is where they can make their mistakes, so they can work effectively with each other to get results. They adopt the name of their online persona on the play deck. It makes things simpler."

"In the assembly, why did you let Eclipse off so lightly compared to Polycrates, especially when it produced such a bad reaction?"

"Surely you know the importance of theatre, Mr Vaklerner? All the children know I know everything already. They've got mandatory daily blogs, and they all inform on each other all the time. No one ever suggests leniency: that's why I sometimes use it to shake things up and get a reaction."

"What did happen at the end of the assembly?"

"I don't need to have been there to take this. You've been curious about how we fund this school, Mr Vaklerner. You must know that some of the best teachers only have to cast a glance to get control? Well, it doesn't get better than the Miss's withering stare. That stare's how we keep the school open, thanks to a select group of CEOs out there."

"Once they're in the zone, it's immaterial whether I've got the capacity to follow any of it up. Confidence is the key thing in business, after all. Two on my books meet the threshold for this school and need an occasional top up, but the rest only require one short meeting. That's why I stood in front of you at the end of the assembly. You must surely have realised by now that our children often turn up having done the impossible? The flip side is that anything is possible. Without my stare we couldn't have opened this school in the first place. I wanted to show you we can control the children if we decide to work together. Polycrates' confession was real, but Eclipse was working with me to get them riled. Helped me reassert my authority. They don't like it when I use my stare, but most of them realise it's useful for their understanding to defer to someone in their lives."

"And the data dashboard I mentioned earlier helps stamp out collusion to promote effective collaboration. Luckily, they're all keen to inform on each other, which keeps the system ticking over nicely. I'm glad you're getting a fuller picture, Mr Vaklerner, but time is against us. Now you've had an overview of our school, what do you want from us?"

Valentine took his time to respond, reflecting on his visit. Now he understood why Dinners had persuaded Front to send him here. But he still wasn't sure he could trust them. They all had the habit of pulling the rug to unsettle him. But perhaps this was their way of maintaining a professional distance so things didn't get cliquey. He tried to cut through his residual doubt.

"Why am I really here, Ms Scape?"

"Why are we all really here, Mr Vaklerner? I presume you realise we can give your ministry whatever makeover it needs?"

"And Spads Grant and his team?"

"We can help their visions reach fruition … in any time-scale you wish."

"I'm not here to shore up the Ministry for British Schools, am I?"

"What do you mean, Mr Vaklerner? We haven't got the time to talk in riddles. If you've got another question, you'd better ask it now."

"What about taking on Front at the same time?"

Valeria smiled.

"A higher level player. Of course, Mr Vaklerner. We were always going to give you the support you asked for. Now we're even more invested in helping you. The networking children are already working on the anti-bullying project. Now I can give them something that'll really test their metal. I thought our school might be called on to do something inside government at some point. I'm retiring soon, and Miss won't be far behind, so I'm grateful in a way for things being so awful. But I do have some bad news for you personally."

"Bad news? I'm used to bad news." Valentine said this as nonchalantly as he could.

"Well, here it is. We'll need your reputation as collateral damage to make it look convincing."

Valentine felt a bit punch-drunk, and it helped him respond.

"Why not? I've already endorsed the anti-bullying initiative on film without knowing what it was. But do you think you can do it? Isn't he a bigger problem than he seems? Sorry, another question. Do you think he would have got into this school if it had existed back then?"

"Not sure. I crossed paths with his mother once. She might have got in. But I can't call it. That's what makes it interesting. If we're lucky, he won't be much more than an attention-seeker who'll be useless in a real crisis. We'll have to play our cards, including you, skilfully to find out. The good thing in our favour is that Hebden has been onto him from the start. He's one of those exceptional people every organisation needs. He sensed trouble way ahead of anyone else, soon after Pleasant Drivelling became an MP. Even the hair and the name were Hebden's creations."

Valeria had put down all of her guard by now.

"You see, Mr Vaklerner, Hebden's hope has always been to create a big enough dislocation to change the rules of the game. That's why the Prime Minister needs to be on the verge of his biggest triumph yet. Make sure you're ready. It's going to be a roller-coaster ride."

There was a heavy knock on the door.

"Code clean green," Valeria shouted through.

Dinners peeped around the door wearing a mischievous grin. "Ah thought ah'd get code greenwashin' with this one."

"I'm fully on board, Mr Hamble. You can dial down the caricature from now on."

"Ah'm made up for ye, son, but ah'm a method actor, me."

"You're in safe hands, Mr Vaklerner. To make you feel better, my stare even works on the most advanced robots. And

I'm not retiring until Persephone perfects hers. Then the future's sealed."

"So nothing to worry about, then?"

"Ay-aye lad!"

In safe hands

1

Just when Valentine thought he had some allies, something odd happened. He took a call which began by asking him if he was having a super nice day. Another misdirected sales pitch for Spads, he thought. Spads liked to shop himself out of his problems, especially with public money. And it helped to keep him occupied with doomed projects like schooling toffees to chew in and out of lessons. This was his response to criticism that bullying was much more than physical contact with a plan to stop children talking to each other.

Then Valentine thought it was another prank call. Was there someone else in the background? Despite all the filters, they were getting quite a few of these across government. But he wasn't expecting the nerve of this prankster, calling him to an urgent meeting at No.10. Yes, of course he could be there in an hour.

"Thank you for being so super flexible, minister. It would be super helpful if you could be here in thirty minutes."

He played along. If it was really urgent, happy to help, but he'd need transport.

"Super urgent, yes, transport, yes, thank you so much min …." Valentine thought he heard laughter in the background.

"We're super organised – already sent a car. Better still if you could be here in twenty minutes."

Then the call suddenly ended. Was this a scam? It was too equivocal to be Dinners role playing. And he'd recently delivered Valeria's case studies straight to the Prime Minister himself, keeping his special advisers out of the loop as instructed.

He'd even supplied the messaging. *Getting radical with schooling* was the motivator for parents to accept a step change in school discipline, backed up by Valeria's data showing a corresponding step change in schooling outcomes. Valeria's second case study was more subtle than a straight U-turn. It could also be used as a reset once schooling outcomes settled at a higher level. *Lighten up about schooling* fronted the second data set showing the advantages of a less hot-housed approach to school behaviour. He knew there was no place in this re-imagined world of schooling for someone who had taken school discipline too far.

Having delivered on the government's most radical policy hack to date, he wasn't going to be ruffled by this prankster. Someone somewhere was trying it on, and Valentine decided to do nothing to smoke it out.

2

Half an hour later Valentine was sitting in a room at No.10 waiting for his urgent meeting. Someone had helped the Prime Minister bump him into this, but he felt relaxed thinking about Dinners and his unusual school, and consciously made his body language reflect his indifference to any outcome Front had planned for him.

All the same, he sat facing the door to maintain his guard. He wasn't surprised to be kept waiting now he was here. Front was reassuringly predictable. When the door handle moved and the door stayed closed Valentine smiled, reflecting on the ritual humiliation always built into his interactions at No. 10. More minutes passed before the door handle moved down and stayed there for a few seconds until an unfamiliar face entered the room, still glancing backwards until Front followed him through the doorway.

Before any words were uttered, Valentine sensed he was in for a good cop bad cop routine. While the Prime Minister was glowering at him, his partner fixed him with an inane smile. Front's new sidekick was unlike any one Valentine had encountered before at No. 10. He looked like a creative of some sort with his t-shirt, distressed jeans and untied shoulder-length hair. Interestingly, it wasn't clear from their interactions who was the master and who was the servant. Front's sponsored haircut had lasted longer than anyone would have expected, thanks to the extended virtue signalling gifted by Dinners' fictional narrative. He'd reverted to a regular hairstyle long ago, but his back combing and the smell of hairspray suggested a tragic effort to look cool alongside the younger man.

Inertia took hold of the moment. Valentine enjoyed projecting his quiet confidence, the stranger strained to keep flexing his ambivalent smile and Front was fidgeting, becoming more brittle by the second. Then the stranger turned his head to look at a vacant seat at the table. Front jumped and darted out of the room, returning at breakneck speed carrying a thick red cushion which he placed carefully in the middle of a chair.

Front checked his partner was comfortable before he sat down opposite Valentine.

"If this is about schooling, shouldn't Dinners be here?" Valentine asked to push Front's buttons from the get-go.

Front snapped back. "I'll ask the questions here, know-it-all. This is Percy Klepthappy. I don't want to embarrass him, but this man totally gets my can-do vision for this country."

Percy Klepthappy didn't look embarrassed. Front took off; destination unknown.

"Percy agrees we can't afford not to include kitchen and bathroom pledges in the next manifesto. He likes my idea of making kitchen and bathroom development a government ministry in its own right."

Klepthappy concurred. "I never realised the general state of the country's kitchens and bathrooms was so super depressing."

"I'm thinking of opening a government-backed kitchen and bathroom showroom on Horse guard's Parade." Front seemed unaware he had raised his hand like a child in a classroom when he said this. Was he thinking aloud, or was he being serious?

"Super exciting, Prime Minister. A new kitchen and bathroom for every family every ten years."

In their budding bromance, Front and Klepthappy seemed to have forgotten there was someone else was in the room.

"Wouldn't that mean delaying delivery until after the next parliament?"

"Who asked you? Don't you understand anything? Home improvement is what voters really care about, so we get a higher percentage vote from a higher turnout at the next election. ...and years to execute a U-turn if we can't deliver. Have I got that right, Percy?"

Front was all over the place, vacillating between dominance and subservience without the professional boundaries Dinners maintained in his own idiosyncratic style. Valentine knew all too well that Front's ridiculous behaviour could only be dismissed in the abstract: underestimating his capacity for causing chaos was crude entry-level analysis in the current context. Klepthappy seemed to appreciate the need to calm things down, and backed up Front with a slow nod. Valentine was tired of waiting for this urgent meeting to get to the point.

"Perhaps you called me here to talk about next month's schooling launch?"

Front bristled, but his partner returned serve.

"Pleased to meet you know-it ... Yes, it's not long until Christmas Eve, so we thought you'd appreciate a face to face meeting to be super clear about the PM's launch of his schooling revolution."

"You can manage out Grant: we're handling all the comms here. Don't mess up this time, Vaklerner. It's going to be really Christmassy, isn't it, Percy?"

"Yes, Prime Minister. That's why we're going with a super kids' winter party theme."

"And I can star in my very own advent calendar?"

"Yes, you can have your super advent calendar."

"And people won't mind only three lottery winners if we give out enough bouncy castles?"

"Of course, Prime Minister. We've only made a thousand of our super collectable government-backed kids' winter party-themed bouncy castles. We're super lucky to have a visionary like you, Prime Minister."

From Klepthappy's obsequious delivery, Valentine understood he was looking at a fully engaged player. Some industrial-scale dabbling would be required for the Prime Minister to steal all the limelight of the schooling revolution. Now Valentine could see Klepthappy's game – doing the heavy lifting for now as the ultimate yes man, until Dinners was usurped and cast aside.

3

Klepthappy then showed a bit more of what he was made of, giving Valentine an overview of the Christmas Eve launch they were going to drip feed through the accompanying advent calendar. They had concocted a bizarre brew of mashed up memes. The opening scene was a magical winter castle, entered through a Parliament-style portcullis to reveal a cavernous kitchen/recreation space, crowned by an industrial-sized kitchen peninsula.

"Kitchen peninsula?"

"Who wants to be marooned on a kitchen island?"

"You're so right. I'm trying to keep up."

Children's schoolbooks strewn over the marble effect work surface. Front skipping in as Santa, with his arm sweeping the books off the end of the kitchen peninsula into a row of accessory matched pedal bins. Santa gambolling over to a notice board, removing printed off e mails about a parents evening and a homework club. Scrunching the e mails into paper balls and disposing of the old world through the kitchen's basketball hoop. Back to the notice board: picture of two best friends on their first day at secondary school. Cut to an article about one of the pair, placed in detention for playing football on their twelfth birthday. Over to a bookcase full of impressive volumes, then through dry ice remembering the day shelves had to be cleared to make way for years of copying out from the new curriculum.

Front was lapping it all up, looking so smug Valentine felt duty bound to have some fun.

"Are you still going to be the nation's favourite storyteller reading from the cracking new schooling curriculum?"

"We're making serious changes here; it's not children's TV!"

"So you don't want the special armchair we've project-managed for you?" Klepthappy shuddered at the mention of a special armchair.

"Another half-baked idea!"

"But the junior schooling advisers have been working flat out to get it just right."

"Stop wasting my time!"

"They've had committees working on the upholstery finish."

"THIS IS MY MEETING. LISTEN TO YOUR INSTRUCTIONS AND SHUT – UP!"

But Valentine wanted a little bit more.

"Why don't you try being nice to everybody, Prime Minister? Don't be not nice to anybody."

The gravitational force of the Prime Minister's ego was bending political space time too far. He was visibly vibrating, taken to the event horizon of another temper tantrum when challenged by someone he perceived as a threat.

Valentine enjoyed projecting his nonchalant expression across the table. He mused on what success had done to the Prime Minister. He must have had a reasonable skill set to claw his way to the top. But his attempt to close down Valentine in front of his new favourite was backfiring. Klepthappy used the opportunity to close off the meeting.

"We've improved the new schooling lottery draw. We're even going to have the winners on the set at the Christmas launch."

Was Klepthappy being serious? Valentine upped his concentration.

"The draw's taking place forty eight hours earlier and we're giving the winning families a day at a rehearsal boot camp."

"Will a day be enough, Percy? What about the other children?"

"What other children?"

Hadn't they planned more children into the government-backed kids' winter party-themed TV launch of the most radical changes to schooling in a generation? Valentine played it cool.

"Children might go quite well with a kids' winter party theme, Percy, especially because it's about schooling."

"Do you think so, Mr Vaklerner? Aren't children too random for the level of finish we're aiming for?"

So he was Mr Vaklerner now, was he: was he finally being taken seriously by Percy Klepthappy?

"I do know where you're coming from, Percy. This is a new level, even for the Prime Minister, and it needs to be on point from start to finish. What if I can source a group of children who can be rehearsed perfect for the launch? They could turbocharge the public's attitudes towards the Prime Minister and his team."

"Carry on."

."Here me out here, Percy. The children from the school that's given us the anti-bullying case studies are more than capable of making the launch unforgettable across the entire electorate. I know they can be as good as the children from any theatre school."

"How much rehearsal would they need?"

"I think they could meet your exacting standards in a week or two."

For the first time Percy Klepthappy looked out of his comfort zone, and cast an alarmed glance at Front emerging from his stupor. Valentine enjoyed watching Klepthappy's window of opportunity disappearing in front of him.

"Let's do it." Klepthappy had just made an executive decision he might live to regret.

4

"This meeting isn't over until I say it's over."

Front must have recovered enough to remember running away from their last meeting. He stood up to stand his ground. But the main business in the room had been concluded without him. And Klepthappy didn't help with his mime about an urgent message, followed by a quick exit. How was the Prime Minister going to belittle Valentine Vaklerner without his audience of one? Who was going to protect him from Vaklerner's off-piste questions? The power dynamic wobbled. Front slumped down on his chair with a thud. (He could have done with Klepthappy's cushion.)

But Valentine didn't have any more questions. He enjoyed sitting behind his blank look, finding succour in Front's manifest imposter syndrome, especially now he'd secured more opportunities for Valeria's children to work their magic on the schooling revolution. Long seconds ticked by until a junior staffer opened the door.

"Fire! Fire!" they shouted as the din of the fire alarm took over.

The relief on Front's face was palpable. The fire alarm meant he wasn't running away from Valentine this time. His trip on the carpet was to be expected under the circumstances. Valentine exited the room calmly, as per the protocol.

He found himself in a crowded corridor shuffling towards the smell of smoke. (No. 10 was such an illogical place.) He wasn't surprised to be at the back of a queue, shuffling far too slowly: he could see smoke now. He made a determined effort to stay calm as the air became more acrid. Despite his long career, Valentine had never been in a situation like this before. But there was something familiar about it. It reminded him of staff rooms before the smoking ban. He remembered the office stress that hit at the time. It smelled like smoking. Had someone been smoking in here? He had to walk past a closed office door that seemed close to the source of the problem. Why weren't there enough fire doors at...?

What Valentine couldn't have expected was to be on the receiving end of some kind of rugby tackle; pulled into the danger zone, and slumped down on a chair opposite a chain smoking Dinners.

5

"Have you done this? I didn't know you smoked?"

"Ah don't. 'avn't got long, so shut up an' listen."

"No. All I'm getting in here is shut up. You listen. I've met Klepthappy and I've persuaded... "

"LISTEN!"

Dinners stared at Valentine with an impersonal look that was like a peek behind the gruff artifice at a cold and serious intent. It had the desired effect.

"'e found out ah drove ye t' the school. 'e don't know it was me own school yet, but 'e's keepin' us on a tighter lead. Ah'm only out of 'is sight in 'ere when 'e's plottin' with Klepthappy."

"Klepthappy wasn't very impressive in my meeting. He didn't even realise they needed children fully involved in the launch. The good news is I've persuaded him to do just that."

"SHUT IT, MAN! Ah didn't get ye moved t' Schools f' nowt. SHUT YER CAKE 'OLE AN' LISTEN!"

Valentine had only recently formed his opinion of Dinners as a political force of nature, so finding out his career had been sunk by the man himself was hard for Valentine to take, especially on the back of another encounter with the Prime Minister. But what tipped him over the edge was receiving this revelation while being told to shut up and listen – again. And he could see straight through Dinners' chain smoking. More method acting to achieve the desired outcome.

"NO, YOU LISTEN! I've got you to thank, have I, for being forced into this parallel universe? I could have challenged Front again as Home Secretary. Instead, I've had to humour these schooling hackers on a daily basis, while my civil servants think I'm a fruitcake!"

"Ye bloody fool. Ah've extended yer shelf life a bit longer than 'e planned! 'avn't ah showed ye some interestin' stuff to 'elp ye go out with a bang? Try t' work with us, Val. We're both in too deep t' bottle it now."

Whatever the truth of the matter, Valentine knew it was too late to walk away now.

"Carry on, but get into your skull the fact that I've just levered your school properly into the live Christmas launch, so NO MORE SHUT UP AND LISTEN!"

"What dye want? A medal? Ah counted on ye to get more kids in there. Dye think ah'd take any old Whitehall drone t' visit me school? Ah persuaded Front not to 'ave any kids at the kids' winter party launch. Wasn't 'ard. 'e 'ates sharin' the limelight. Klepthappy took some o' the bait t' spite us. Brought forward the LIVE lott'ry draw to 'ave some kids in there. Bloody fool.

But don't underestimate 'im. 'e's a first class opportunist. When ah used that dissolvin' chair on 'im 'e fell on 'is arse, ev'ryone was laughin' at 'im, it bought us a bit o' time, but 'e turned it 'round. Started usin' 'is red cushion. 'is arse isn't sore any more, but 'e's still usin' it. Tells people, "the super power be'ind t' throne needs a throne too," be'ind Front's back. Can't tell Front owt about 'im durin' during the 'oneymoon phase."

"Surely the children at the launch will make mincemeat of Front and Klepthappy?"

"That depends on you, son. Spads' lot'll be 'istory by Christmas, but if Front gets a whiff we're in on this together … That's why ah need t' look ye in the eye an' ask ye 'ow far we can embarrass ye?"

Valentine had said yes when Valeria mentioned ruining his reputation to make Front's fall look convincing. He soon realised this was partly a reaction to the limitless possibilities he perceived during his visit to her school. His non-reptilian brain wasn't averse to falling on his sword if it helped the country turn a corner. Whoever was left to take over couldn't tinker around the edges: they would have to take on changing the whole political culture. But did he have to be humiliated at the live Christmas Eve launch of the schooling revolution to get there? Wasn't there another way to topple this political supernova from the top of the tree?

"Time's up, Val. Ah need yer answer NOW."

Dinners started to cough, again and again. The atmosphere created by his chain smoking was disgusting, but Valentine knew he was opposite a real player who could have decided that coughing in his face was the best nudge at this point. He wasn't going to be bumped into this.

"You've been by his side for years. Isn't there any other way?"

"Look, ah gave up me teachin' to do me activism 'ere. Ah created Front, bin closer to 'im than any one else up t' now, an' look at the damage 'e's still done!"

"So, I'm expected to end my political career in public disgrace so you can atone for your own mistakes?"

"Oh Val, ah thought ye were better than the rest of 'em! Don't ye realise if it's this bad now, 'ow bad would it be if ah wasn't 'ere tryin' t' contain 'im? If that Klepthappy takes over – well, there's only one way down a bloody worm 'ole."

Valentine didn't come back at this because he hadn't been told to shut up and listen again, and because he knew in his gut that Dinners was right. He'd seen many examples of poor organisational culture in his time. More often than not, it came from the top. He thought about the multiverses of dire consequences that existed where Dinners hadn't created Front to try and manage him, where Pleasant Drivelling or whatever he would have become could act without any restraint at all. This was the world Percy Klepthappy was promising to the Prime Minister. Dinners rambled on, suggesting the possibility of some genuine tension underneath the method acting.

"'e got 'is unrealistic expectations from 'ow 'is mother runs Domesboroughton. But 'e's diff'rent to 'er, loves the limelight, doesn't micromanage everythin', likes bein' on t' edge o' bein' found out. Thinks it gives 'im 'is appeal. But 'e does 'ave a big weakness, an' that's bein' the centre of everythin'. Ah'm sure it's the best plan f'r 'im. 'urry up, Val. 'ow much can we scapegoat ye t' keep it real?"

Valentine knew there was only one appropriate answer to Dinners' question. The graffiti camouflaging the school's entrance popped into his head. He remembered the philosophy hiding in plain sight, possibly a code. It took him to an ancient wisdom – only a fool would aim for the top of the tree. The trouble was that Front was comfortable there. His addiction gave him a superhuman grip, and he was the master of giving very little back to anyone else. He could defy political gravity for years ahead. He could define an irreversible era. Perhaps Dinners' school was the best chance of a cure, especially now its children were going to be fully involved in the Christmas launch. But was he prepared to put himself completely in their hands?

"Go for it. Happy to help."

"'bout time. Can't stand much more o' this!"

6

Valentine thought about the meeting he was under strict instructions to complete today, and winced. Dinners had insisted that Cosmina had to be the one to liaise with the school. Just as well, because she guarded her research role like a warrior. But even telling Cosmina something she'd want to hear wasn't straightforward. If it wasn't happening inside the cells of her monster spread sheet, it wasn't real for Cosmina.

Involving Spads wouldn't help. He was visibly pining for his old access to No.10, which had been withdrawn by Percy Klepthappy. This was a body blow to his epic mission, and he was merging into the amorphous mass of the junior schooling advisers for comfort, ditching his Edwardian motorist garb for superhero office dress down. Spads hardly ever spoke to Cosmina any more, the best way to avoid being confined to his office on another detention.

Valentine's walk across the open office in his own ministry shouldn't have been an event, but the reaction of the junior advisers made it one. He could feel all eyes on him as he knocked on Cosmina's office door. And as he walked straight in, he heard a thud behind him. Had someone fainted?

"How's the schooling research going then, Cosmina?"

He took his weak intro from Valeria's admission interview, to confuse his worthy adversary.

"Schooling – research – is – my – business." Cosmina fixed him with a particularly withering look.

Valentine jumped, hoping for a soft landing at the end of his free fall.

"Something's come through about the anti-bullying research that's so urgent; I thought I'd better bring it directly to you myself."

"Speak." A good sign.

"I know you're inspecting the volume covers for the new curriculum tomorrow, but No.10 have finally signed off on the school to back up the anti-bullying initiative. It's a boarding school with excellent staff accommodation, and they're expecting someone from Schools to join them for the work to start tomorrow. How would you feel if Spads went instead of you, so we don't mess around with your diary?"

His calculated risk to produce a short circuit appeared to be working. He knew Cosmina wouldn't want to let Spads in on her territory. And his hunch she wouldn't differentiate between criminal sanctions and the design of a book binding might be correct.

"Research is mine! Get the school to postpone for forty eight hours!"

"They won't postpone. If we don't start tomorrow, they'll pull out."

"Then – find – another – school." Cosmina fused aggression with condescension. But Valentine had read the trajectory of this encounter right so far, and played a card he'd deliberately held back until the cogs in Cosmina's brain were rattling.

"The anti-bullying initiative's a big ask, Cosmina, and this school is perfect. I've done the due diligence myself. I've even persuaded No.10 to let it help us with other parts of the schooling revolution at the Christmas launch, like Spads suggested."

"THAT – WAS – MY – IDEA!"

Valentine knew it was Cosmina's idea. He was there when she said it. But her contempt for him and especially for Spads produced a reaction that blew her gaskets for a few seconds, giving Valentine his best chance.

"We're not going to get another school past No.10 on this time-scale, Cosmina. I know you're in charge of research, but we have to send someone tomorrow. I'd prefer that person is you, but we do have Spads. His diary is much clearer than yours."

"You can't send him without me." The ice was cracking.

"Should you both go? That can be arranged."

"Spads is too busy online shopping. Reschedule the print run."

"AMAZING!" Valentine's involuntary reaction put him on alert. Had Cosmina noticed? No, she hadn't.

"Excellent. I'll let them know. A car will collect you at six tomorrow morning."

Valentine gestured to make a quick exit, then winced when he remembered Dinners' final instruction.

"You can call me Val, by the way."

"What's the name of this school?"

But Valentine was already closing Cosmina's office door behind him.

7

With Cosmina safely dispatched Valentine was left with Spads to manage, a relatively straightforward task now that No.10 was ignoring him. Spads had regressed into the petty office gossip in the open office space. He was always looking for ways to criticise the acting senior junior adviser's work ethic, and his annoying habit of meeting a deadline.

"He doesn't know what he's talking about. Has he thought that through?" Spads seemed to have forgotten his belief in the power of inexperience.

Valentine had to stop himself pitying the increasingly needy Spads, remembering the chaos his brainwaves threatened to unleash on the nation's schools. There was still some residual compassion, however, which manifested in his indulgence of Spads' policy fantasies, a much easier task now he knew they had nowhere to go. Dinners wasn't disturbing him, trapped as he was at No.10, and enough of a player not to put any faith in telecommunications. So Valentine decided he had some space to play in preparation for the trials ahead at the Christmas launch. And with Cosmina ignoring his messages, Spads was daily at Valentine's door.

"Can I bring forward our meeting, minister?"

"We're meeting at ten, Spads. Can't it wait until then?"

"Ideally, no, not really. I'd like your opinion on something to see if it's worth taking further."

"You're right, Spads. Today's idea might be one. Take a seat."

"I know Cosmina's working on this, but I might have invented something to make the bullying initiative run more smoothly."

"You mean the anti-bullying initiative?"

"Every school needs its own school jail!"

"What? You mean beefing up exclusion units?"

"No. I mean a jail, a proper prison cell on the school site. Look at this. It's a flat pack made from reinforced cardboard. I've got a supplier that could send every school its own detention centre in the post!"

Valentine expected a back-of-the-envelope sketch, but Spads handed him a photograph of a box with its own barred window and secure door with hatch.

"Are you sure this is a good idea, Spads? Remember parent reaction to the chanted rules at the disciplinarian preschools?"

"These jails are for secondary schools, minister."

"Sorry, Spads. You're right. I'm trying to keep up. Well, what about this? Make it an opt in to each school's behaviour policy. Ask for parental authorisation to place their child in the school jail."

"That's an excellent idea, minister. A few parents opt in at the start. We use some of them as advocates, and then there's a rush to opt in. Soon everyone agrees if school jails didn't exist they'd have to be invented."

"I think you might be onto something here, Spads. Two-tier school behaviour policies, giving parents an element of choice, might go down well with No.10."

Although there was very little of any policy substance germinating between Spads' ears, Valentine had to give him credit as a talented shopper.

"How you package it is the key thing."

"I'm thinking of an instruction film for school caretakers."

"You're a bit behind the times there, Spads. You mean school facilities management? But I meant how can you reel in No.10 while keeping control?"

"What about this? Make it a place to stay overnight. Children can complete their sentences on the school site."

"No.10 will like that, Spads. It could take pressure off the prison system. It could even allow you to start making things up inside the Home Office. Mr Grant, you might be making the anti-bullying strategy truly sustainable."

Spads was in clover. Valentine let him savour the moment before nudging him back to a kind of reality.

"I hope your cardboard boxes are waterproof, Spads?"

Spads contorted his seating position.

"What about toilet facilities?"

Spads threw his pencil across the room. How was he going to act out his schooling brainwaves if he kept having act outages?

"I think you've got a bit more work to do on this, Spads. No.10 won't tolerate mass breakouts on rainy days. Remember, we can't take ideas to the Prime Minister if we haven't thought them through. We need to give him his exit strategy from the start, we need to hold something back to keep some ownership, and then we need to look at it all again to plan getting around Klepthappy. It's complicated."

"OK." Spads was nicely deflated, so Valentine moved things on to real business.

"We need to be extra careful what we feed No.10 before the launch. Especially once Cosmina finally gets back from her school visit."

"Oh, you're right. We need to control the school's input at the Christmas launch." (It really helped that, despite their daily meetings, Spads never thought to ask Valentine the name of the school.)

"Now you're getting it, Spads. I for one don't want to see the Prime Minister stealing your entire schooling revolution from under your nose."

Spads nodded manically: when his penny dropped, it was easy to think he was a mechanical device.

"Yes, minister. We need to keep our schooling revolution in safe hands."

"I couldn't agree with you more."

8

The next anyone heard from Cosmina started with a call from Reception. Reception apologised, knew he was busy – he wasn't particularly – but it would be best if he came down to sign in the two visitors himself. Cosmina Blame didn't have the required level of authorisation.

Valentine was surprised Cosmina was returning to the Ministry with members of the school. She had gone completely under the radar for nearly two weeks. After the first week he was getting plagued by calls from Klepthappy, whose love bombing of the Prime Minister chopped and changed the launch schedule, and required everyone else to be thoroughly hassled. With Dinners still off the scene, Valentine had no way of communicating with the school, and he was only buying time with blatant fob offs. Who was with Cosmina today, confident they could manage her within the confines of the Ministry for British Schools itself?

"Thanks for coming down to Reception, Valentine. I know you're very busy, but we thought we could catch up some time if we all met here together today."

He couldn't see who was waiting on the other side of the security barriers but, more importantly, who was this person being courteous to him? It looked like Cosmina Blame, the clothing was just as austere, but the change in manner was so stark he wobbled. Did Cosmina have an identical twin sister?

"Who are you? ... Who are you asking me to sign in today?"

"It was going to be Miss Class and Iphigenia, but Miss had to stay at school, you know, to do her thing. So Valeria's come instead. Thanks again for coming down to sign them in."

He wanted answers, so ploughed them through the necessary admin and ushered them into a lift. Cosmina broke the silence as they were nearing their floor.

"I'll get out first and create a distraction."

Two minutes later Valeria and Iphigenia were sitting in Valentine's office. Their arrival had hardly been noticed. The first question was obvious.

"What's happened to Cosmina? Who is this person?"

"You tell him, Iphigenia. You were there at the start."

"Hebden wondered about Cosmina, so we tried her out with Persephone as soon as she arrived. We'd taken over an annex in one of our partner schools. Persephone showed Cosmina around making mistakes all the way and getting corrected by Cosmina every time, pretending to be upset at first, but then pushing back. Cosmina got more aggressive at first, but she mellowed when Persephone really challenged her. We thought Hebden might be onto something, so we put her into a no holds barred interrogation with Miss Class, which she passed..."

"In eight minutes," Valeria added.

"… and the result is the team player you met this morning."

Valeria took over. "No one had stood up to Cosmina like this before, and we uncovered what was really going on with her. She'd given up on finding someone to measure up to her high expectations. When she encountered Mr Grant she was treading water supply teaching, which was easy with her behaviour management skills. She thought she might be able to mould him into something that could make a difference, but he picked up and ran with all the oppositional curve balls she threw at him. So she settled into general provocation, strutting around on the off chance she might find someone with the guts to say no to her schooling brainwaves. By the way, she doesn't blame you for this mess. She fully understands the position you're in.

Hebden thought she had potential, and he was right. Plan A was for me to boss her around horribly, telling her all my orders came from schooling Val, and setting up some off-piste activities for the children she wouldn't be aware of behind the rehearsals she was in. As it is we're on Plan B. Cosmina's fully in the know. She's giving Spads an update of sorts, and then she'll join us."

"Aren't you both taking a big risk coming here like this?"

"Don't worry, Mr Vaklerner. With so many new schooling initiatives, we're both of us ancient history."

There was a gentle knock on the door and Cosmina entered.

"I've given Spads something to keep him busy. I've told him this is the last piece of the puzzle needed for the Christmas launch. He's trying to work out how transition to secondary school can take account of when children actually turn twelve. He's excited about the comms opportunity – a new schooling policy that completely turns the tables to help children born in

July and August. I've told him we need a strategy for the oldest children who'll be subject to criminal charges for bumping into each other within weeks of starting their new secondary school. I've told him to report back to me alone. Let's see if he can resist the temptation to spill the beans to No.10. By the way, I'm still bossing him around horribly. He couldn't cope being treated on a level."

"I do worry about Spads when Front gets bored with the schooling revolution. This Whitehall ego trip's made him almost useless."

"Don't worry. He'll find something."

"Let's get back to why we're here, shall we? Anything to say for yourself, Cosmina?" Valeria pointed at the notes Valentine had kept on his whiteboard as a reminder of the exceptional schooling times they were in.

Help every lesson – copy out that text
Help teachers with assessment – sign off that copying out
Help teenagers to behave – don't break the law

Cosmina said nothing, but emitted a mischievous grin.

"This shouldn't take long, Mr Vaklerner. Here is our information for No.10."

The heavy A4 envelope Valeria handed over was securely sealed at both ends.

"Should I give this to Dinners?"

"Really not necessary, Mr Vaklerner. If Percy Klepthappy saw it first it could help along his hubris. By the way, all the late changes he made to the schedule are accounted for in here. You should know the children are even more motivated to help you now. They're furious the government is trying to use unnecessary home improvements to win the next election. I've signed off all of the improvisations myself, if that makes sense? We were able to decant back to school once Cosmina came over to us. You'll find out our roles as the day elapses to keep you fresh. You should have Hebden to support you inside the launch bubble. I can't imagine Front excluding him from this. I'll have to be back at school because Miss Class is involved in the plans. It's an unexpected bonus to be delivering this to you in person today, though I must say a final visit to the Ministry for British Schools wasn't on my bucket list."

There was a knock on the office door: probably Spads, who'd have to wait. Another knock on the door, and then a surprise: a civil servant with a message for Valentine to take the urgent call flashing on his desk phone, and then a quick exit. Civil servants rarely broke cover to bother him. It must be important, so he apologised and took the call. He soon regretted the decision, and it showed.

"Is something wrong, Mr Vaklerner?" Valeria asked.

"The endgame's started. That was a call from HR at No.10. They're claiming to help, but it's really about processing me out."

"Try to see this as the final visual, auditory and kinaesthetic learning experience of your ministerial career."

Valeria wasn't helping. Reassurance was what Valentine needed now.

"So how *is* Front going to be pushed over the parapet?"

"You know it's best we keep that from you, Mr Vaklerner. You'll be physically safe, but we need it to look spontaneous. Secrecy is the only way to keep it real."

That wasn't what Valentine wanted to hear, and he felt his nerves coming back with a vengeance. But he was in too deep to do anything about it. They were placing their trust in him, so he'd better look as though he was holding it together. Valentine had to make himself believe he was in safe hands.

"I totally understand. Is there anything you *can* tell me?"

Iphigenia read his discomfort. "I've never seen Persephone as motivated by anything as she is about this."

"She won't lose it, will she?" After his call from HR, Valentine was finding it hard to shake off a negative frame of mind.

"Here's the thing. Persephone mellows when she's amongst civilians above ground. You should know that we've taken the kids' winter party theme very seriously in our plans."

"Kids' winter parties have become a bit of a national tradition."

"Sadly, so have kids' winter party scams."

Happy to help

1

Was there any hope at all for a country whose Prime Minister shouted down all objections to him playing Santa Claus on live TV to launch his latest vanity project on a bewildered public? Valentine had railed against his insomnia to perfect the foul mood he was in, standing outside an anonymous warehouse at stupid o'clock on a freezing Christmas Eve morning. He spotted Spads, who was camped outside the single door cut into the metal wall of the building like someone determined to be first in the queue at a Boxing Day sale. He was hunched up in a foetal position inside a superhero-branded sleeping bag, clutching a coordinated thermal mug. He looked awful.

"Wake up, Mr Grant," Valentine shouted down at him. "What are you after? You've already got the matching mug." Spads jolted awake, oblivious.

Then Valentine jolted himself as the warehouse door opened with a creak. A security guard stepped outside and gestured for them both to step back and form an orderly queue. This was much easier for him than for Spads, who was so desperate to follow instructions he forgot about his sleeping bag. He fell onto the floor, panicked when the zip wouldn't release him, and eventually stepped out of his cocoon shivering and dishevelled. The guard made no allowances.

"Move further back, sir," and to Valentine, "keep a ten metre gap, sir. No listening in."

Ten metres? Valentine soon understood why when he witnessed the drama at the front of the queue. He saw Spads handing over his security pass with a gesture of entitlement that didn't last long.

"What? Finished off with a felt tip?" The guard was being serious.

Spads suddenly stood bolt upright in a light bulb moment. He took a phone out of a pouch in his superhero rucksack, dialled a number and handed it to the guard. The guard filmed his performance for nearly a minute - all to no avail. Spads appeared to be losing it so the guard suggested something, twice, to pierce through his tantrum fog. Spads pulled out his crumpled suit jacket and the guard filmed a more dignified charm offensive this time. But a shake of the guard's head floored a stunned Spads, who was carried off by two more security guards who emerged from the warehouse. Where was he being taken to? At that moment Valentine didn't really care. He needed to get out of the cold, so quickly presented his own pass and was waved through.

Dinners greeted Valentine on the inside. "Yer gonna need extra make up, Val. Ye look awful."

"What do you mean? I'm not front of house tonight."

"Ye know this winter party's goin' off-piste."

"Just testing. Do you know about Spads?"

"Can't 'ave 'im claimin' it's all 'is idea, can we?"

"You know it's not totally his fault. He got elevated too high too fast. You should have seen him being carried off. I do feel a bit sorry for him."

"Don't waste yer time worryin' 'bout 'im. 'e's too good at landin' on 'is feet. Look at 'ow 'e got No.10 out o' that boot camp nurseries mess. Robot 'eadteachers were 'is idea: contained most of the parent fury 'e unleashed 'imself. Front was losin' it so we kept the worst of it from the 'ome Office. Did a deal with a grandmother from Barnsley t' delete 'er *'owsitcomet'this* 'ashtag. Couldn't 'ave put it better meself!"

Dinners cracked the briefest of smiles.

"'oo'd 'ave thought some scammer gave Grant a fake security pass? Don't worry 'bout 'im. Y've got plenty on yer own plate."

"Don't remind me. But why bring me here this early if I can't know the details to KEEP IT REAL?" Valentine didn't like being sarcastic. He blamed his two hours of sleep.

"Oh Val, ah'm disappointed in ye. Ah want ye t' see the bairns settin' it all up."

"What? Final rehearsals?"

"Much more than bloody re'earsals. 'ere they are."

They felt the chill of the entrance opening, and a group of ten young children in retro uniforms carrying bulky cloth bags filed past them in silence. Valentine spotted Persephone amongst them, looking every inch the wide-eyed child starting their first day at secondary school. Miss Class followed, dressed like an austere governess.

"Younger bairns f'r the bullyin' 'ack."

"You mean the anti-bullying hack?"

"More bairns back at base with Iphigenia n' Cosmina, overridin' the live delay an' gettin' reactions from our 'and-picked social media influencers. Klepthappy thinks 'e's directin' the 'ole thing. Wants t' steal me job f' Christmas. Doesn't realise 'e's even nearer the door!"

"Do you think we're going to bring an end to this foolishness today?"

"Done everythin' we can, Val. Can't make it look like a bloody coup, can we?" Dinners was exasperated by Valentine's need for reassurance.

"Somethin' t' calm ye down. First thing in t' other Val's instructions. Time-locked security bubble. When yer in ye can't get out 'till midnight. Says t' safeguard the bairns, but it's really t' stop the adults gettin' away before the bairns've finished with 'em. Let's 'av a look."

Valentine and Dinners walked onto the vast set, three of the four stages eerily bare, not in any way like the magical winter party billed in the TV schedule. Only the kitchen set was recognisable. The children were in there, fixing a hosepipe from the kitchen sink to a network of smaller tubes. Their collaborative focus finally gave Valentine the reassurance he was looking for. Dinners didn't mind. He needed the Minister to have a clear head to play his part.

"Let 'em get on with it, Val. They've got a lot to do before the production crew get 'ere. Good news is phones don't work in 'ere. Put yer feet up. Comfy Christmas sofas on the way. Christmas caterin' in the boxes over there."

"Shut up, Dinners. Spare me the sales pitch."

2

All credit to Dinners, Valentine thought, as he witnessed Front's protracted arrival. He knew his subject all right, and saw the dangers this man posed before anyone else. Front arrived just after 5pm, an hour late but already dressed in a Santa Claus suit. Klepthappy trotted along behind, noticing the magnificence of the now-completed sets – his design – and looking like someone about to receive an award. Unfortunately for the new chief adviser, the Prime Minister wasn't sticking to the script.

"Where's my box, Klepthappy?"

"I think we left it in the car, Prime Minister."

"YOU left it in the car. Go get it. NOW!"

So Klepthappy was fair game for public humiliation, Valentine observed. It looked like Front's latest clique wasn't lasting very long. The Prime Minister didn't seem to care he could be overheard by the production crew. They had been awestruck by the beauty and intricacy of the winter sets when they arrived after lunch. Front's strop gave him tunnel vision. He didn't register the sets at all.

"They won't let me out," whined Klepthappy, returning empty handed.

"RUBBISH! SEND SOMEONE ELSE IF YOU'RE TOO PROUD TO BE MY GOLFER."

"Is he drunk?" Valentine whispered to Dinners.

"Only on mince pies. Look at 'is beard?"

"They won't let anyone out. It's the security bubble." Klepthappy's voice was wobbling.

"WHAT'S WRONG WITH YOU? TELL THEM I'VE AUTHORISED IT!"

"You're right. Santa's cooking nicely."

"'arder t' switch on the charm when the cameras roll. Can ye see 'is stooge swayin'?"

Klepthappy was at a singularity. Despite all he'd done he was being humiliated in front of yesterday's men. Keeping the Prime Minister happy risked wasting more time he couldn't spare. He had no choice but to find a backbone.

"No one can override it, Prime Minister. It's part of the agreement to protect the children. It's called safeguarding."

"WHO AGREED TO THAT?"

"The school insisted on it. We ... you agreed."

"CALL THE DRIVER. SHE CAN BRING IT IN."

"Phones have gone down in here."

"EXCUSES! DO I ALWAYS HAVE TO DO EVERYTHING MYSELF?"

There was a moment of collective shock: had Klepthappy been slapped? But it was only the bagginess of Santa's sleeves as he swirled around to sort things out at the entrance.

Klepthappy tried to pretend he'd dropped something, but wry smiles all round told him his deflection wasn't working.

"'e's got a lot more antagonistic since my time, son."

"***!"

Dinners theatrically wiped a fleck of non-existent spittle off his right cheek. He was in a very good mood now, and he let out a belly laugh when he spotted what was returning, an even more dishevelled Front incommunicado inside another temper tantrum, suspended between the security guards who had despatched Spads at the entrance. One handed over a red ministerial box. The other explained.

"We made an exception because he was charging the door and hyperventilating. Is there a responsible adult who can take charge of him?"

"That's a question we all ask," Dinners replied.

3

Less than twenty minutes now until the kick-off at seven: star and director were still not back on set. Valentine and Dinners knew Front could take too long to emerge from his tantrum and might miss the whole thing. Valentine was worried and also annoyed because Dinners didn't look particularly bothered. Dinners certainly had nerve: the fate of his Westminster mission was at stake and he was in a carefree party mood, entertained by the children's send up of their rehearsed routine on the opening set. Valentine dragged him to Front's trailer with a *KEEP OUT* sign hanging from the door handle.

"What are we going to do?"

"Wait."

Five minutes later and still no sign. Valentine was getting agitated. They looked back towards the children, who now showed signs of restlessness. This triggered Dinners, who started hammering on the trailer door. No response. They walked around to the back of the trailer and there they were, deep in conversation sitting on a comfy sofa. Klepthappy appeared to have retreated to his comfort zone; telling the PM exactly what he wanted to hear, even if it risked the whole shebang. At the sight of Klepthappy's indecisiveness, Dinners finally snapped.

"Get on that set NOW an' meet the bairns yer dependin' on," he bellowed.

Klepthappy couldn't hide his relief. "Perhaps a final pre-brief on the set, Prime Minister?"

"Get my cue cards, and DON'T BE LATE," bellowed Front as he marched off to makeup.

Despite his recent trials Klepthappy was sticking to the party line. Yes, Front was going to use his cue cards. Too much preparation made the Prime Minister stale.

"What's keeping him?" Valentine's nerves were never far away.

The answer was obvious when they caught sight of him. The Prime Minister's hat and wig looked like a festive attempt to rekindle the shock of his dramatic debut on the national stage.

"What do you think? Good, isn't it?" Front wanted his glory reflected back on him immediately.

"Now yer 'ead's really in the clouds."

Valentine got the deflecting punch. "I hope these children of yours know their lines?"

"They've been in final rehearsals since early this morning, Prime Minister. Don't you think you should meet them?"

"What's the point of that?"

"A bit of team building before you go live?"

"They're not voters, Vaklerner."

"Can we all gather around now, children? Here's the super treat you've all been waiting for. Your chance to meet Santa before we launch the schooling revolution you're super lucky to be trying out first today."

Klepthappy looked pleased with himself, but the children didn't say anything, downloading data.

"Ahoy classmates! Are you ready for big surprises at my super new Christmas school?"

Still no reaction from the children.

Valentine broke the tension.

"Let me introduce Miss Class, Prime Minister. Deputy head of the children's school."

Front didn't have a card for this.

"Tonight, Miss, we're going to launch the biggest changes to schooling in a generation. I hope your children are ready?"

"They know what they have to do, Prime Minister, and they know their lines. DO YOU?"

Miss blunted her stare with an equivocal smile, but she'd done something to the Prime Minister who threw his cue cards across the floor with some force. The blood drained from his face, but it was too late to cause another commotion.

"Remember, children, you need to look like you're running up the steps of the magic winter castle as fast as you can, but you must let Santa stay in the lead at all times."

5, 4, 3, 2, 1, and they were on. Santa went for it. The children indulged him, skipping up and along the steps, swapping sides in a tight formation that actually met Klepthappy's confusing instruction. They had clearly rehearsed very well to allow Santa to be the first to enter the impressive winter castle where the schooling revolution would be unveiled. Unfortunately, over-competitive Santa got beyond himself and tripped up the naughty steps. The children improvised to maintain the spectacle and, when Santa staggered under the portcullis last, they were all already in position ready for scene two.

4

Santa staggered into the next scene with a sack of fake presents on his back. Even though the gift wrapped boxes were empty, he didn't have to pretend to overexert himself.

"Cosmina's gettin' froth off social media. Why put a kitchen showroom in a winter castle?"

The state-of-the-art contemporary kitchen/recreation space in scene two was vast; the only part of the set finished when they'd arrived. It had a giant kitchen peninsula with a row of ten stools screwed to the floor along one side. The children were already perched uncomfortably on the stools with piles of schoolbooks in front of them, all looking thoroughly miserable as per the script. Santa surveyed the scene with the steady dependability of a superhero. (Spads would be pleased.) A melancholy violin played for a few seconds, and the children began their lines.

"We hate homework."

"Why do we have to do homework?"

"We only have homework because we waste too much time at school."

"Why can't schools be better?"

"So we don't have any homework when we get back home."

There was an awkward pause before someone remembered their line.

"Don't worry. I'm going to do something about that for children everywhere, not just you lot."

"Can you do our homework for us, Santa?" That wasn't in the script.

"Show us how much you care for us, Santa. Can you help me with my homework first? PLEASE?"

Persephone held out her exercise book and pen. It was written on her face that Santa was going to come to her rescue. Santa had to accept the challenge while working out what to do and made some notes for a few seconds, before handing the exercise book back to Persephone, who took her time to examine his efforts forensically. Santa smiled. This was going to work.

"LOOK WHAT SANTA'S DONE TO MY HOMEWORK! I'LL GET DETENTION! I'LL GET EXPELLED!"

Some of the other children suddenly stepped up like Special Forces on a mission, using a torch and some mirrors to reflect Santa's homework efforts onto the sleek chrome fridge's shiny surface at the very moment Cosmina's team overrode the cameras to focus on his words for the audience to see.

STICK TO THE SCRIPT. PLEASE!

The children had landed their first glove on the Prime Minister's image. It was game on. Valentine and Dinners were glued to the action on the set. They both knew that inside this entitled, attention hungry self-publicist stirred a political survival instinct that got him to where he was today. Political nerds rarely got so close to the excitement of a football match. Percy Klepthappy was walking around in circles like the fan who couldn't handle it and annoyed everyone else. What was Santa going to do next?

As expected, Front still had some of the old magic when he found himself in a pickle. Santa used one of the corners where the kitchen peninsula joined the kitchen mainland to lever himself onto the marble effect work surface using his padded belly. He stood up on the counter and started to kick the children's books along towards the far end of the peninsula. He wanted his unscripted frenzied kicking to look both comical and urgent, stressing he was still that man of the people who could ride to the rescue when the chips were down. The children cheered to prove his point, and he kicked the books off the end of the kitchen peninsula shouting, "no more children's tears, no more parent stress with that time consuming project or that impossible maths."

It was all suddenly going so well again. Cosmina reported social media fashion influencers going wild about kitchen peninsulas doubling as home catwalks. Dinners looked glum. But someone had moved the homework dustbins Santa was expecting to fill over to the far wall. The hardwood floor was covered in the children's books. A bit more of the real Prime Minister surfaced.

"Which of you lot did that? Hurry up. Own up. Stop being so childish."

"But we ARE childish, Santa. We're children. You're the only grown up here."

"CLEAR IT ALL UP. TAKE RESPONSIBILITY, ALL OF YOU!"

"We're not here to swap homework for tidying up your kitchen, Santa. Get someone else to sort out your mess."

Santa froze with an uneasy calm that often preceded a tantrum. Klepthappy's arms were flapping, but he wasn't panicking. He was trying to calm Santa down. He switched to an even more exaggerated flapping gesture with a beaming smile on his face, and it worked. The stakes kept getting higher, but Santa managed to keep up.

"You're right, little girl. The Minister for British Schools is here. He can help. Would you like to join me for the next exciting schooling surprise over there?"

"Cheeky…," but Valentine suddenly found himself in front of the cameras, shoved there by Dinners to clear up Santa's mess. He had two seconds to get back some dignity before the cameras panned to him.

"Here is our Minister for British Schools taking personal responsibility for consigning homework to the dustbins of history. Do make sure we keep our schooling revolution nice and tidy, Mr Vaklerner."

Valentine was in turmoil, but kept to the unseen script he'd signed up to with a broad smile.

"No probs, Santa. I'm always happy to help."

5

The live broadcast they were trapped in had had a troubled birth. Front wanted breaks in his high energy schedule, so vetoed using the state broadcaster. Dinners intervened once the government had signed a contract with a major commercial channel. He planted a fertile seed with Klepthappy that the maestro shouldn't have his wings clipped by an advertising break. As a result, the government had paid big bucks to secure thirty uninterrupted minutes of prime time commercial TV when they could have gone to the state broadcaster in the first place. Two scenes in and Front was suffering the consequences. He was flagging in his boil in the bag suit and itchy headgear. Apart from regular shouting and flexing his superficial charm he did little exercise, so running up winter castle steps and schoolbook football had nearly winded him. He staggered to the kitchen noticeboard in such physical disarray he temporarily forgot the schooling revolution was all about him.

"It's too high. What does it say, Santa?" Persephone pulled at his sleeve.

"This one is about a homework club. We won't be needing that any more. And this one is an e mail about a parents evening. We won't be needing that either."

In his reduced state Front focused mindfully on small details, taking both sheets off the notice board and replacing the pins carefully. He could have had forty winks there and then, but Persephone shocked him back to fight or flight mode.

"Oh Santa, I want to believe all your lies. I really do."

Front froze. He was frustrated these moments kept occurring in his political life. Someone usually stepped in to help him out, but he couldn't get Klepthappy on set and Dinners would tell him to ... He couldn't outsource responsibility this time. He had to find his own way out. He happened upon human interest as a good bet, especially with a child.

"You haven't told me your name, little child."

"I've been told not to give my name to strangers."

"Not even to Santa?"

"Not even to Santa Claus."

"Don't you believe in Santa Claus?"

"I do believe this Santa Claus is unbelievable."

He changed tack to make it about him. He must be recovering. He wasn't interested anyway.

"Not even to a Santa Claus who's going to liberate schoolchildren and their parents from never-ending schooling seeping into homes across the land? Stand back."

Santa scrunched up one of the sheets into a ball and, expecting Klepthappy to be ready with the basketball player stunt double, launched it for all he was worth.

"You missed." A statement of fact from Persephone as the camera panned to the kitchen's basketball hoop, with his forlorn effort landing well short.

Behind the cameras Valentine could see Percy Klepthappy starting to panic, running around in circles. He gesticulated at a camera operator, but all he got back was a shrug.

"Cosmina's technical override," Dinners whispered in his ear.

"You missed, Santa. Does – that – mean – I – still – have – to – do – my – homework?"

Persephone laboured her sarcastic question as a challenge Santa couldn't ignore. He scrunched up the second sheet and threw it with all the energy he had.

"Missed again. Let me help you out."

Persephone retrieved both paper balls before star and director could do anything, hitting two shots through the middle of the basketball hoop with the camera following all the action. There was an awkward pause. This was where the adult was meant to praise the child. Millions of viewers knew this, but Santa didn't.

"Didn't I do good, Santa?"

"And cut." Klepthappy's voice trembled: he'd triggered the short film introducing the anti-bullying scene earlier than planned.

"Look over there, Val."

"Where?" Valentine's eyes took a few seconds to adjust. Then he saw something he understood instantly, the back of Miss Class facing a basketball player who looked nearly seven feet tall but was pinned to the wall looking terrified.

6

Next came something that couldn't veer off plan, the sepia-filtered film about two secondary school friends on diverging paths: one jailed for a football tackle on their twelfth birthday; the other sticking to the rules and eventually partying away at university. Off air Klepthappy suggested Front could use the time out to repair relationships with the children.

"Not before I get another mince pie," was the Prime Minister's statesmanlike response as he stormed off to catering. It wasn't a no so Klepthappy waited patiently while Dinners and Valentine chatted to the children, who had gone straight to their next position, sitting on the kitchen peninsula stools testing out their physical distancing with outstretched arms. Dinners showed he was much more than the sarcastic Whitehall plotter Valentine had become used to, chatting to the children about nothing very much at all, but listening and encouraging all the while. Front returned and fitted into the group without demanding everyone's immediate attention. It was a rare moment. Perhaps he was actually listening to learn something. Klepthappy appeared to be doing the same. He politely asked Dinners to take over. Dinners gracefully gave way.

"All already in position. Well done, everyone. Remember, sleeves up so the cameras can read your government-backed personal age readers."

The children nodded, ready and calm. Front weighed in with his own brand of motivational pep talk.

"Right, you lot, I want it real. Understand? I want to see the emotional journey. And I want to see your gratitude to ME for making it all happen. I hope you've learned how to measure time by now?"

"Oh yes, Santa. We learned that yesterday. I don't think we'll get it wrong today."

Persephone's sarcasm went over Santa's head because she'd told him what he wanted to hear. His scowl evaporated and they were back on.

"Time to *get radical with schooling,* children. Hold up your fool-proof government-backed personal age readers. Well done. Now make sure you speak clearly for the register. And remember to read your reader carefully so we can apply the correct rules. Twelve and over, you've got our new anti-bullying law to help you. No one wants to miss class because they're in jail, do they?"

Front had flipped into role depressingly well.

"My name is Odin. I'm seriously ready to take on my new legal responsibility in 3 months, one week, 4 days, 4 hours, 55 minutes, 36 ..."

"Thank you, Odin. Months, weeks and days would do."

"My name is Gaia."

"No more nicknames on the register, children."

"Gaia is my real name, Santa. Haven't you heard of it before? Where on earth have you been? My government-backed personal age reader confirms I turned twelve 2 months, 2 weeks and 11 days ago. I am maintaining my physical distancing so I don't get blamed for bullying. It helps me complete all of my learning at school so I can enjoy my free time at home."

"Still too much information, Gaia. Next."

"My name is Cybil. I turn twelve in 5 days. I'm ready to take on my no physical contact legal responsibility when I turn twelve to help me do all my ...."

"Thank you, Cybil. Next"

The next few children stuck to the script. Santa improvised some lines about the importance of taking responsibility that triggered a heckle from someone in the production crew. After eight children, half were subject to the new law against bullying and half knew precisely how much time they had before they turned twelve. Santa was on auto pilot.

"Thank you, Maverick. Next."

"My name is Persephone. My government-backed personal age reader confirms I turned twelve 47 years, 2 months and 28 days ago."

"Thank you, Persephone. Next."

Either Santa hadn't noticed or he wasn't giving Persephone any more air time. Klepthappy looked like someone who'd thought the worst was over and realised it wasn't.

"WHAT? ARE YE TELLIN' US YER 59 YEAR OLD?"

Santa did notice Dinners throwing his voice onto the set. He wasn't going to let Dinners muscle in, so took the bait.

"You can't be 59 years old, little girl."

"My government-backed personal age reader is fool-proof, Santa. You said so yourself. It can't be wrong."

Santa's face was contorted by a rapid risk assessment.

"You're right. Our readers can't make mistakes. You're old enough to be a prefect. Keep an eye on the others and arrest any bully who's turned twelve."

"I will, Santa. Thank you for the extra responsibility."

"You're welcome, Persephone. Next."

"My name is Judge. I turned twelve in 1756."

"Happy birthday, Judge. What a lucky boy you are to be here on your birthday."

"Not AT 1756, Santa. IN 1756. Today's not my birthday."

Santa's superficial patience hit the inevitable wall.

"If you can't even read your reader correctly, come over here and let me read it for you."

Cosmina's team overrode the cameras to focus on Judge's expression as he followed Santa's instruction. It was the first time Valentine saw anything that resembled the children in their assembly back at the school. Judge channelled his weary disgust as he held out his arm to show Santa that this child with a brain the size of a planet hadn't got it wrong.

"See, it says I was born in the YEAR 1756. I'm the oldest person here!"

The camera fixed on the console on Judge's wrist and it confirmed he could have been around during the French revolution. Santa didn't hesitate.

"Congratulations, Judge. As the oldest person here make as many citizen's arrests as you judge necessary to keep our Christmas school safe."

"Thank you, Santa. I won't let any get away."

"Excellent. Now line up over here, children."

The children left the safety of their physically-distanced kitchen peninsula stools and, in tribute to the danced football of Spads' vision, followed Santa over to the kitchen/recreation space bookshelves, exaggerating trying to avoid physical contact all the way. As the oldest children by far, Persephone and Judge kept their eyes peeled for any rule breaches. There were none as the children lined up in perfect single file. Then someone sneezed, the children bumped into each other and the prefects made four arrests, leading the twelve-year-old miscreants in a caterpillar mime of mixed emotions to a row of Christmas-themed prison cells on the adjacent stage.

Dinners tracked the convict transportation but Valentine stayed put, speculating about what had just happened. Spads probably went behind Cosmina's back to share his latest brainwave with the Prime Minister. Front probably threw money at it to come up with the government-backed personal age readers as his own idea. The malfunctions suggested two main possibilities. A rushed government IT project, or the school having a hand in the manufacture of the readers. Whatever the case, Valentine was impressed by the final sting, invoking that unwritten rule: leaders don't blame the IT when they can blame people. Did the children know the Prime Minister would rather say a child was hundreds of years old than do a hand break turn on a malfunctioning IT system? The political activism specialists probably did.

7

Over at the bookshelves Santa had reverted to mime, moving his hands slowly along the shelves to reinforce the impressiveness of the rows of volumes stacked there. Klepthappy was back in control of the cameras, and cut to a close shot sweeping across a complete set of the cracking new curriculum for British schooling, with numbered bindings from early years to secondary graduation year.

"AND CUT." They had a sixty second breather during a film montage explaining the new curriculum, standardised lessons and no exams at the end. "Make space on your bookshelves for your child's copied out learning. Everything they need to know for the rest of their life."

On paper this was the most straightforward scene; a re-imagined Santa's grotto easily accommodated inside the vast kitchen/recreation space where the Prime Minister would become the nation's favourite storyteller, revealing a perfect new curriculum that guaranteed success for all. Santa slumped into his tastefully ill-matched armchair next to the home library every home would soon have in the retail renaissance about to sweep the country. Santa was joined by Persephone, Judge and the other children who hadn't been sent to jail, excited about the next treat in store.

"Listen, you lot. This is a different kind of story time, so make sure you look interested and STICK TO THE SCRIPT."

The children all smiled back. "10,9,8 ..." They were finally shaping up, he thought. "7,6,5 ..." His mind wandered onto the lottery draw coming next. "4,3 ..." He was comfortable and relaxed. "2,1, BACK ON."

"Santa, can you read to us from the new curriculum for British schooling?"

"Of course, children. What subject would you like me to read?"

"Can we have some geography? We like to understand the world around us."

Santa was liking this. The page was bookmarked. This was an easy win.

"Here's something called human geography for children your age. *It is very important that out of town shopping developments include a certain mix of outlets, which sell a variety of products from everyday essentials to one-off purchases. Everyday essentials includes ...*"

"This is boring, Santa. Can you tell us a different story?" This wasn't in the script. Santa soldiered on.

"Everyday essentials include sweets, snacks, fizzy drinks ..."

"Are you sure that's right, Santa?"

"Haven't they heard of healthy eating?"

"Who wrote this Christmas curriculum cracker?"

Front instinctively understood that his current predicament precluded a total loss of control. Better to act like a normal Prime Minister playing Santa Claus on live TV.

"Children, lets..."

"I'd ask for my money back."

"We really must ..."

"Perhaps it's a test to see if anyone notices."

"I don't think that's what..."

"Can you copy out something that makes sense, Santa? Show us how lessons should be done."

"I'd like to, but I don't ..."

"You can borrow my pen, Santa."

"And the minister gave me an exercise book from his homework dustbins as a souvenir."

"Ooh, isn't that dirty?"

"No it's not, Santa. It's an empty exercise book. I don't like telling you this, but you were kicking perfectly good resources onto the floor. Don't you know it's a terrible waste to throw things out like that?"

"Shall we rescue other things from the bins, Santa?"

"Do you want to help us, Santa?"

"Shall we ask the minister to help us, Santa?"

"ALL RIGHT! I'll find something to show everyone how the new curriculum is going to work. Every volume has an index showing the exact topic every year group should be following in every lesson every day across the academic year. All the different subjects are interwoven through each year, so everyone in a year group will study the same subject at the same time. Oh, and every teacher will be able to teach every subject as long as they know how to find the correct copying out."

Santa looked pleased with himself. How did he remember all that without his cue cards? Dinners shrugged. But the unscripted questions kept coming. He had to continue this rally with more than one player on the other side of the net.

"Will these volumes fit inside classrooms, Santa?"

"Yes, every classroom will be its own library."

"Don't we need more tables, Santa? Remember, we can't sit next to each other when we turn twelve."

"Take out the desks to physically distance and fit in the volume of the volumes." Front liked his ability to turn a phrase.

"Can we take out the chairs too, Santa?"

"We can work on the floor, Santa."

"I'm not doing that, Santa."

"We can work standing up, Santa."

"Look, Santa, I can hold a volume like this and put my exercise book on top. I can change arms when it hurts."

"Where will all the volumes of our copied out work go, Santa?"

Front was relieved to turn his back on the children and face the bookshelves, pretending to search for a volume.

"Here, I've found something. Let's have that pen and paper. I'll show you how it's done."

He knelt on the floor to use the seat of his armchair to pretend to copy out something from the volume he had selected at random.

"There you are, see how easy it is? We don't want to be late for the grand draw of the government's new schooling lottery, do we?"

"I didn't see it, Santa."

Judge snatched the exercise book out of Santa's hand. Persephone took a lamp off the bookshelves that turned out to be an overhead camera, overriding the other cameras to share Santa's latest efforts for all to see.

WHAT DO YOU WANT TO STICK TO THE SCRIPT?

The vision froze, but not the audio. A disembodied exchange boomed across the set.

"No more homework."

"YOU'VE GOT THAT."

"No more exams."

"THAT TOO."

"No more teaching."

"THAT COULD EASILY BE ARRANGED."

Santa flopped into his armchair, pretending to read his volume of the cracking new curriculum. A holding position: he was sitting it out to let his minions sort it out around him. But Valentine and Dinners were close to permanent exclusion from the government, and Klepthappy was flapping about another technical malfunction. Luckily, Persephone moved things on the moment the malfunction ended.

"No more sulking, Santa. No need to be sad. Children should be allowed to have some fun at a kids' winter party. We can't be late for the grand draw of the new schooling lottery. Let's walk there together while I tell the audience what you forgot to tell them about university being another big party. Do you like parties, Santa?"

"I like a well behaved party." Valentine knew by bitter experience what that meant.

Persephone let out a giggling shriek of delight. "On behalf of all the schoolchildren in this country, we just want to say a big thank you."

8

"'urry up, Val. Get a move on."

Dinners could move quickly when he wanted to. Valentine was forced to break into a light jog to keep up.

The smell announced the next scene first, followed by some smoke. Valentine was glad they'd arrived first to see star and director's reactions to the completely off-script thank you the children had put on for Santa in his winter castle's throne room. Christmas arrived early for Dinners. Valentine loved what he saw, Klepthappy catching sight of the Christmas BBQ the children had put on for Santa a few seconds before Santa himself. Within the grandeur of winter castle's throne room the Christmas BBQ was a grim affair, like an extended family of campylobacter had arranged it and invited guests. Miss was cooking the not very festive-looking fare, replete with low voltage stare.

"A Christmas BBQ is not a British tradition."

'You're wrong, Santa. That's what it says in the food technology section of the curriculum cracker." A thought flashed through Valentine's brain. "That's how the acting senior junior schooling adviser met all his deadlines. He simply wrote anything!"

There was smoke everywhere and it soon became clear why. The children were throwing mince pies onto the BBQ. Judge tried to create a party atmosphere.

"The Ministry for British Schools has helped us set up this special surprise for Santa because IT'S CHRISTMAS!"

"I'd like to see him get out of this one," Valentine whispered back to Dinners.

"Watch out, Val!"

Valentine had to steady himself as two greyhounds wearing antlers and greyhound-friendly grey boiler suits pushed past him onto the set. He had a clear view of Santa looking stunned: the substitute reindeer instantly replaced the Christmas BBQ as his top concern. But wasn't the Prime Minister meant to like background chaos? Didn't it give his interventions their edge?

"Couldn't let 'im miss out on live TV with children AND animals, could we?" Valentine turned around. But Dinners was looking more pensive than pleased.

"GET THE MINISTER ON HERE! NOW!"

"NOT AGAIN?"

"'fraid so, son."

"CATCH 'EM, MINISTER."

Santa suddenly had an opening.

"Look, children, the Minister for British Schools won't let his reindeer spoil your lovely bar-be-que." Santa laboured his delivery, smiling at Valentine's discomfiture.

Valentine found himself shoved back in front of the cameras, flailing around on live TV. He felt like prey in a Roman arena. They told him he'd be physically safe. Was that a nudge to get him to where he was now? It would be greyhounds, not the easiest dogs to catch. To make matters worse, he saw one of the dogs trying to relieve itself on the set before running away when he got too close. He just had to go for it, and when he accepted how ridiculous he looked he cornered one of the dogs, guiding it off the set by its red and white collar.

Dinners was there behind the cameras to collect the greyhound, which lay down on some kind of non-verbal cue. Valentine turned around to go back and finish the job. At least that meant he could get away from Dinners. He'd had enough of having the carpet pulled from under him today.

"'old on, Val." Valentine yanked his jacket collar out of Dinners' grip with a force that was noticed by members of the production crew.

"Don't bother goin' back, Val. Trust us, yer never gonna catch t' other one quick enough."

"What do you mean?"

"All ah can say is may need a wee!"

The greyhound still at liberty soon obliged, taking a comfort break on the corner of Santa's throne, then following Dinners' summons. What was that fizzing noise?

"I hope this has taught you a lesson, children. Always ask for permission from a grown up first."

9

"Lottery winners ready?" Klepthappy took charge, but director and star had another surprise to contend with. An unscripted lottery draw cloud descended into the throne room, accompanied by a booming fanfare no one could ignore. Klepthappy had to perform something like a rugby tackle on a camera operator to keep the lottery winners out of shot.

"Can I draw the winners, Santa. Can I, can I?"

Santa had to think fast.

"No, you need to be grown up to do this, Persephone."

"Are you grown up, Santa?"

'Of course I am. I'm the adult here. You're the child. You need to do as you're told."

"What if I'm not grown up enough to do as I'm told?"

"Listen, you should be old enough to understand the word no."

"But I'm 59, remember? I could be older than you are, Santa."

Santa shuddered, trying to pretend it was because of the winter fog starting to drift across the set.

"I'm the oldest. I should draw the winners."

Judge reached into the cloud, pulling out small circles, triangles and squares. Santa's adrenaline rush gave him an opening.

"You need to know your squares from your triangles and your circles to draw our exciting new lottery. Put them back in the cloud and let's start again. Have you learned your shapes yet?"

"Oh yes, Santa. And I passed a shapes refresher test only yesterday."

"Well done, Judge. Draw out a square first. Well done. Now draw a triangle. Persephone, you can have a go. Draw out a shape that doesn't look like the shapes in Judge's hand. Well done. Your shape is called a circle."

"Thank you for that, Santa."

"Let's have your shapes, children."

Santa's next set of hurdles hit him. Were the names he'd been handed the real winners? Even he didn't expect to be that lucky. How was he going to check? And how was he going to explain welcoming the lottery winners onto the set? He jolted bolt upright with another inspired idea.

"All the lottery finalists are waiting in the banqueting hall next door. If you and the other children clear away the lottery cloud, I'll go and collect them. I'll announce the winners when they get here."

Front felt pleased with himself. He didn't need his cue cards after all.

The square draw winner wasn't a very promising start. Leos was painfully shy. He would only communicate through his mother. What new school did he want to go to? Leos wouldn't name one. His mother wouldn't name one either. She explained they were a musical family. Leos was named after her favourite composer. His current school had an outstanding music department. They were entered in the lottery by mistake. They tried to withdraw. The school even tried to help them. They didn't want a new school.

But Santa wasn't moved. Life's not fair. Leos had to change schools. See, it wasn't so difficult, was it? If Leos would stop crying he might enjoy his fresh start. Mind the puddles. Mother and son were led off the set by two children, stunned by the lottery winner rendition they'd just been subjected to.

The triangle draw winner was a bit more on-message. Lucky had really enjoyed being a schooling lottery entrant. She loved wearing her *I want better schooling* sweatshirt, knowing her teachers had to accept it as correct school uniform. She demonstrated how she absolutely loved strutting around her primary school, performing her own dance on the set with arms akimbo, wildly kicking around the foam now covering the floor. But Lucky wasn't sure she wanted to change schools at all, now that her school was shaping up so well for her. And she wasn't worried about her meeting with the headteacher on the first day of term. She'd sort things out. But her parents stepped up when it mattered with a quiet word, and Lucky named her new school.

Valentine had a double take when the circle draw winner was announced. He recognised Theo straight away, looking at the floor as he shuffled through the sludge. And this must be Oliver, visually carrying the weight of the world on his shoulders from his strict academic regime. Did Valeria have to make Oliver a lottery winner to buy Olive off? What sort of mincemeat would Olive make Front into? But where was Olive? They started without her, and Theo started to find his voice. Yes, Oliver could choose any school he wanted. Yes, he could go to his personal choice, a selective sports academy – he was good enough to get in after all. Theo then stole the show with a speech about schooling that sounded very carefully composed over time.

Front basked in Theo's reflected glory, with Klepthappy switching shots between father, son and PM. After a long pause, Oliver named his new school. Cosmina confirmed that a wave of emotion was melting the social media audience, which had a strange parallel in the decay of the set. Father and son walked off the set slowly to keep their balance on the slippery floor.

"I saw this family interviewed back at your school. Where's the mother?"

"Big 'oo-'aa between 'er an' Lucky at yesterday's re'earsals. Lucky put 'er on detention. Or was it in detention?"

But at that moment their attention was pulled back to the action on the set. The children hadn't cleared away the lottery draw cloud, as Santa requested. They'd been taking squares, triangles and circles out of it, placing as many shapes as they could onto their open palms. All squares had Leos' name, the triangles Lucky, and the circles Oliver. And when they realised the cameras were on them, they shouted in unison.

"Someone's cheating. It's a scam."

10

The cameras cut to the Prime Minister trying to hide inside his Santa Claus outfit. Klepthappy couldn't look.

"'ere we go." Dinners rubbed his hands together in anticipation.

It was hard to tell what was playing out on the Prime Minister's face. He couldn't have got to this point without some talent for escapology, but he'd outsourced his workload for so long, surely he'd gone a bit stale? Long seconds ticked by and he was still computing an exit strategy, shielding behind a mask of self-regarding amusement that the live broadcast had come to this.

"I was going to save this special announcement for the next election, but I think it's only fair to share it now, so voters also have a special present from my government this Christmas."

The Prime Minister was looking more fired up than wound up.

"We will be launching a new kitchen and bathroom policy in our manifesto for the next election. Every household across the land will have the right to a new kitchen and a new bathroom every few years enshrined in law. We're sure we'll get a fresh mandate from the electorate for our new social contract with consumers. But we want to give families across the land a chance to fast forward themselves into their best future. The first ten thousand who log onto a new website on New Year's Day will get a free new bathroom."

Dinners was the best barometer at hand and *he* looked uncomfortable with Front's latest exit strategy. There was a problem with the plan. He upped his concentration.

"Will it 'ave a power shower?"

"Yes, they all have power showers." Front didn't flicker an eyelid.

"An' a bidet?"

Front realised it wasn't Klepthappy and didn't even bother to respond.

"I'm a leader who isn't afraid to level up with the people. Life is a lottery. People need to be realistic about what they should expect from any government. But don't worry. We're committed to giving voters more and more chances of winning a wider and wider range of jackpot prizes."

Cosmina reported social media was going wild. Front was pulling off his most audacious political stunt all on his own. The schooling revolution was already being discounted down to the bargain basement. Valentine felt numb.

"It's not s' bad." Dinners was rationalising.

"'e's like a star that's used up its ayedrogen. 'e seems brighter than ever but, believe us, with pledges like that disaster's not far off. Could be a bumpy ride, though."

The bumps started immediately.

"Emergency!"

"What? Where?"

"It's a disaster!"

"What is?"

"Destruction of the planet!"

"What planet?"

"Is 'e on?"

"Shut up, Dinners."

"How can you live with yourself, Santa? Causing all that waste?"

"What waste? What are you talking about?"

"Ripping out all those baths and sinks and showers that don't need replacing. All that waste."

"All that landfill."

"How are you going to pay for it all, Santa?"

"My festive piggy bank, of course."

The children had had enough. They'd given Santa enough chances. Persephone turned on a temper even Miss Class might find hard to control.

"You stupid man, we can't keep consuming faster and faster, expecting someone else to pick up the mess. Don't you believe in conservation?"

Valentine and Dinners were hooked. Front's latest U-turn looked destined for the political U-bend. If he thought he could blandly smile out this one, he needed to think again.

"ANSWER ME! NOW!"

"I do, little girl. I'm a leader who conserves aspiration."

Wrong answer.

"Then get your festive piggy bank to pay for this!"

The cameras locked onto the children running to the kitchen. They pulled out filled buckets from the cupboard under the sink and returned to soak the walls of the throne room. If the fizzing, steam, foam and sludge gifted by the school mascot's comfort break had remained a winter sideshow, the now disintegrating set couldn't be ignored.

"CUT!"

It was Klepthappy doing something unexpected; making an independent decision and following it through. He was often blown off course by his people pleasing, but he still had a capacity for strategic action to save his own neck. He'd somehow managed to pull the plug on the whole launch, even overriding the override from Cosmina's team. The monitors showed the 1970's test card was being broadcast, accompanied by a manic techno beat.

Klepthappy ran up to Front to work out an exit strategy. Dinners pulled Valentine's sleeve and they followed, pretending to offer assistance to get close enough to hear. With the cameras off, Front was incandescent.

"Get me out of this mess. I'm being bullied!"

Klepthappy's face lit up with a brainwave. "Why not use the super new anti-bullying law yourself, Prime Minister?"

"You're right. These children have used up all their excuses. After all, some of them are older than me. A citizen's arrest could be popular. I used to work with a think tank that was all for that sort of thing."

"How can you arrest them? You can't make physical contact." Valentine was always happy to help.

But Klepthappy wasn't going to be derailed. "Make it super official. Do it in the kitchen: show voters what they could get if they keep faith in the government."

"In ME you mean?" But Front was processing. "I'll shout them back into line."

"Shouting sounds super cool, but isn't bribing them with Christmas presents better?"

"I like it! Behave and get presents or misbehave and go straight to jail."

"Y've just cracked school be'aviour policies. Go on, son. Show 'em what yer made of."

Front and Klepthappy looked taken aback but pleased by Dinners' unexpected approval. Valentine read him better. Dinners was suppressing his delight.

11

When the broadcast resumed they had already decanted back to the kitchen set. The children were sitting at the kitchen peninsula for a tête-à-tête with Santa on his chosen specialist subject; right and wrong. His sermon using Christmas presents as bribes seemed to be working. The winter castle vandals had been transformed by Miss Class and into compliant young children again. They didn't even interrupt when told that no presents came with a jail sentence in the re-imagined childhood the government was making for them. But when Santa finally paused his monologue and they broke the rule not to ask questions – "boring!" – and when they warned him again about climate change – "oh no, not that again" – the children started to get wound up. That wound Santa up, and he flipped into an irony-free disciplinarian diatribe, expecting his emotion and tone to win the argument.

It didn't and Klepthappy's exit strategy descended into a playground row. Everyone got upset, forgiveable in the children but questionable in the country's Prime Minister. Then there were gasps all round as Santa tried to arrest the children. But his shouting didn't work like it did with the Cabinet. The children scattered, apart from Persephone whose age reader wrist band somehow got caught in the chrome backrest of the kitchen peninsula stool she was sitting on.

"Calm down, it's a citizen's arrest."

Santa's bemused furrowed brow suggested he thought this would work.

"Watch this, Santa."

Persephone responded to her apparent detention by trying to cause as much damage to the kitchen as she could. The kitchen/recreation space was the only part of the set not made by the children themselves, the only part that couldn't be dissolved and hosed down the drain. Persephone took advantage of the difference. The noise from kicking her sector of the kitchen peninsula to bits was a bonus. Judge saw the potential and joined in the demolition well out of reach.

"Ah think Judge 'as reached 'is final judgement tonight." Dinners' enthusiasm was infectious. Where was Klepthappy? They couldn't see him. But there were still a few more cold desserts left in this particular meal.

12

Miss Class let long seconds tick by before she intervened. Her safeguarding responsibilities didn't extend to the Prime Minister, even one as immature as this. As they were broadcasting live, she kept her mesmerising stare on a short wavelength, so only her target could see.

"What were you thinking of, Prime Minister?"

Front raised his hands in surrender, but immediately realised this implied culpability and wriggled to get free.

"I may have broken some rules, but I haven't done anything wrong." Front didn't seem to see the irony in his latest excuse.

Miss Class instructed Persephone to sort herself out, which she quickly did and ran off giggling.

"Thank you for letting our children be the first to ride your schooling roller coaster, Prime Minister. But it's been a long day. The children are tired. It's nearly their bedtime, and they need their rest to enjoy Christmas Day tomorrow. If you don't mind me saying so, Prime Minister, you look like you need a rest too.'

"Oh I do, Miss ..." Front always felt better being offered an outlet for self-pity.

"If I might venture another opinion, Prime Minister, perhaps you've been working a bit too hard?"

"Oh yes, my responsibilities do weigh very heavily on me. It's so hard to get the right staff these days."

Valentine exchanged a glance with Dinners and looked for Klepthappy's reaction, but he still was nowhere to be seen.

"I sympathise with you, Prime Minister. It must be stressful having an international role on top of leading the country."

"What do you mean?"

"Putting on this schooling spectacle on Santa's biggest night of the year."

"Oh you're right, Miss. But a real leader just has to step up."

"I totally agree, Prime Minister, and because you're trying to help children everywhere could I give you a small piece of advice that might help you?"

"Of course, Miss. I always like to check in with real teachers from time to time."

Miss peered over the top of her spectacles.

"Remember, they're children, Prime Minister. You really shouldn't go off the deep-end if they drivel on sometimes."

Deep-end ... drivel. Don't depend on Dependable's drivelling! Front's synapses dragged him back to school, back to his earliest memory of managing his imposter syndrome. He froze on the spot.

"I can see it's all suddenly becoming a bit overwhelming for you, Prime Minister. You'd better come with me."

Miss led Front by his sleeve to the set where the naughty twelve-year-olds were patiently being imprisoned. When they realised they had an audience again, they switched on a choreographed anguish.

"If you release them back into my custody, Prime Minister, I'll make sure they complete their sentences back at school."

Front whispered something.

"What was that? Could you speak up a bit, Prime Minister?"

"I haven't got any keys."

"Don't worry, I'll sort it out." Miss kicked open the four cell doors, making Front look ridiculous as much for forgetting it was only a set.

"Make yourself useful, Prime Minister. Help me line up the children so I can get them home on time."

Even in his reduced state, Front made sure he stayed in shot while Miss made forays off camera to bring the remaining children into view. The children lined up like a weary band who'd been through the wars together. Miss checked their physical distancing.

"What's she up to? No one can get out of 'ere b'fore midnight." Dinners was intrigued.

"Has all the winter party excitement been too much for them?"

"It will have been if I can't get them home on time, Prime Minister."

Front looked uncomfortable again. He knew from personal experience it was going to be a tall order getting anyone out of the security bubble before midnight. But his brain must have been defrosting because he was strategising again. He sent a runner to get security to show he cared about safety, and Miss might take the bad the news from them.

13

When the security guard from the entrance stepped under the harsh lighting on set, the scales fell from Valentine's eyes. It was Iphigenia! Now the performance Spads was put through at the entrance made sense.

"I thought Iphigenia was back at school with Cosmina?"

"Ah lied. Couldn't risk the bubble goin' pop with the rest of us stuck in 'ere, could we?"

Was this unplanned improvisation, or was it plan C? It didn't matter. Front fell for the whole thing. The theatre of the not-to-be-messed-with Miss being told no by the young security guard. The role play between Iphigenia and the children. Her lecture about resilience. They'd have to wait to leave with everyone else. They should be grateful to Santa for giving them this character-building opportunity. Persephone whispered something in Iphigenia's ear.

"Can you help me with something, Santa?"

"Of course. Happy to help."

"The children would like to say their goodbyes. They want to tell everyone how good your schooling revolution really is behind today's mishaps. They want to thank you personally for giving them this unforgettable opportunity, and they want to apologise for the damage they've done."

"Of course. Where do I stand?"

"They'd rather say their goodbyes alone."

Front hesitated. Missing out on the limelight didn't sit well with him at all. But he could use the time to plot another exit strategy.

"They only need two minutes."

"Tell them they've got three."

14

"Don't you recognise me, Prime Minister?"

Iphigenia got in first behind the cameras. She knew he wouldn't recognise her, and not because time was short: his main gaze was within.

"I'm Iphigenia Plant. Remember, one of the twins from the government's failed tougher exams campaign? I was burnt out by the whole thing, dropped out, but now I'm ready for a challenge."

Front had to steady himself, remembering how Iphigenia's actions had ended Hepton Royd's political career, opening up his path to the top.

"That limitless ambition, is it still there?"

Iphigenia took aim at Front's flattery receptors.

"Of course it is. Why do you think I got myself selected for this Christmas schooling spectacular? I wanted to see your political know-how in full festive flow. I want to work with someone who's actually good enough to mentor me, so I've got to go straight to the top. To you, Prime Minister. You look like the most can-do kind of leader this country's ever seen. My ambition is to help can-do people achieve even more. Make them into can-do can-doers. Can-do-doers. Can you be can-do-do too, Prime Minister?"

"Yes, yes, yes. When can you start working for me?"

"Would I have to leave my job as a security guard?" Iphigenia added a hint of coy to her precision flattery.

"Yes, immediately."

"It might be possible if …."

"If what?"

"If you got me into the House of Lords."

The Prime Minister could be a meritocrat when he needed someone to dig him out of another hole. Spads was a case in point. Front remembered vividly when he and Hepton Royd had met Iphigenia. Both politicians had felt eclipsed by her. Why not elevate her from security guard to the House of Lords if she could help him reach escape velocity from this Christmas schooling launch catastrophe?

"You can be the youngest life peer in there."

"That'll do for now, Prime Minister, but I really want a hereditary peerage. I expect a report about it on my desk by the middle of January."

"But ..."
Don't waste my time; make it work!"
"Yes, yes, yes, of course."
The deep stoop of his involuntary bow to Iphigenia jolted Front back to the matter at hand. He certainly wasn't going to take responsibility for this mess, and he needed a steady hand on schooling to concentrate on his latest brainwave, bringing forward the new kitchen and bathroom policy. Dinners was too temperamental these days, Klepthappy had turned out to be another useless yes-man, and Valentine Vaklerner was ... responsible. Yes, it was all know-it-all Vaklerner's fault. He didn't know how to handle the limitless potential of his fearless team of special advisers. He'd visited this school, recommended their children, who couldn't execute a simple plan. Vaklerner was a perfect repository for all of the blame.

"Would you mind sitting in the Cabinet too? I need more of my own people in there."

"Oh, go on, Prime Minister."

"CONGRATULATIONS, NEW MINISTER FOR BRITISH SCHOOLS!" Front wanted Valentine to hear.

"Thank you, Prime Minister. I can make sure you are centre stage for this unbelievable schooling revolution. We can sell it as government rev."

Front was delighted by this, but greedy.

"Can schooling be government rev 2? I want kitchen and bathroom development to be government rev 1."

"Of course, we can sort out the details later, but let's not get side-tracked. The children have nearly finished their goodbyes. Then we'll have less than five minutes of broadcast time left. We need to finish off today's business properly SO LISTEN! Let me take over as the director."

"Consider it done." Front toppled Klepthappy in an instant.

"Right. Now get rid of the current Minister for British Schools. Do it in front of the country, and take personal charge of the schooling revolution – yourself – today."

"Can't I hand it all over to you now?"

"No. I'm directing, remember? And not in this security uniform. It's not the leadership look we need. LISTEN, we can't waste any more of this broadcast. Voters need to see you at the centre of everything to understand who to credit for the revolutions in their lives. You can announce me in the New Year. AGREED?"

"Agreed."

At that moment Persephone was the final child bidding farewell to the schooling launch. Iphigenia pushed Front into the edge of the shot. He would have liked to have more time to plan his final humiliation of Valentine Vaklerner, that rival who made him feel more like an imposter than anyone else. But he was a political mover and shaker down to his Santa Claus boots. He was used to taking his chances when and where he could. The Prime Minister launched into his latest political scapegoating with gusto.

"Thank you for staying with us through all the ups and downs we've put ourselves through tonight to show you the schooling your children deserve, not in a few years as a distant dream, but in months and possibly weeks so we can all reap the benefits. My government is not prepared to waste another minute to liberate you and your children from the endless schooling you've sadly become used to.

To do this, I need a new Minister for British Schools who can sort out the hiccups in our new schooling product, which we wanted to share with you warts and all this evening. As you have seen, we are tantalisingly close to unleashing an historic change in schooling, to put learning back in its proper place and invite children to reject crime from an early age. I take my public duty too seriously to wait until the next reshuffle to make the changes I need at the Ministry for British Schools. I need a minister who can hit the ground running in the New Year to roll out our fool-proof schooling policies. So, with a heavy heart, I must ask my old friend Valentine Vaklerner to leave the stage."

Front beckoned for Valentine to join him. Valentine was too quick for Dinners this time: he wasn't going to be pushed onto the set again tonight. His fall through political space time was coming to an end, and he was determined to extract some personal satisfaction from his final trial. He shouted from behind the cameras.

"To be clear, Prime Minister. You want me to walk onto the stage so I can leave the stage?"

"Yes, yes, yes. Hurry up!"

Valentine ambled on, his head bowed in implied acceptance of his imminent fate.

"I'm sorry to have to do this in front of everyone, but I need someone who can take my schooling revolution properly into the implementation stage. And I'm afraid that person isn't you, my old friend."

"I hear you, Prime Minister, but in a few short months I've transformed a pack of radical schooling ideas into the new policies you've announced this evening. Can you tell me specifically why I shouldn't be the person to unleash these policies on society?"

"Yes, as a matter of fact I can give you a very specific reason from this evening why you cannot be the Minister for British Schools any more, why I need to take personal charge of schooling myself until I can appoint a replacement I can have full confidence in. Earlier this evening two reindeer got loose on the set, causing damage to the dreams of children and parents everywhere. I deferred to you as the minister responsible to catch them and get this national launch of the schooling revolution back on track. And what did you do? YOU ONLY CAUGHT ONE REINDEER!"

Front really didn't need to shout at the end, but it helped. He was parading his sneering impetuosity for all to see. It felt like a decent lottery win, but Valentine wanted a little bit more. He switched on the impersonal air he had used when he floated his idea to switch science for shopping know-how with his incredulous civil servants.

"Would it help my appraisal if I pointed out that the reindeer were actually greyhounds?"

The nonchalant trigger worked. Santa's temper broke free with a force that dislodged his headgear, which crashed onto the floor.

"NO, YOU ARE STILL SACKED!"

Valentine walked off the stage, happy that his final appraisal spoke for itself.

15

Some time had passed. The security bubble wasn't letting anyone out before midnight. Miss was using one of her more arresting stares to calm down Special Forces camped outside the warehouse. They were now waiting patiently.

Inside the warehouse the kids' winter party had become a bleak midwinter. The magical winter castle had gone, replaced by a thin sludge the children and Dinners hosed down drains. Most of the seating had gone. Santa's throne went in a matter of seconds, speeded on its way by collaborative effort from the canine reindeer. Only the remnants of the kitchen/recreation space remained. A tribute to the Prime Minister's latest top priority.

The live broadcast ended hours ago, and the time since had felt interminable with phone signals blocked by Cosmina and her team. Lucky had commandeered Front's trailer for the lottery-winning families and was living her best life out in front, leaving very little landfill with her fly kicking master class on the junior advisers' over-thought armchair.

The only seating left was the row of stools screwed to the ground in a no man's land along one side of the battered kitchen peninsula. Members of the production crew took a break there at first, until Front reminded them who the leader was, and told them to get lost. Klepthappy eventually emerged from hiding in the toilet and sheepishly perched on the stool furthest away from the Prime Minister, talking shop with his new Minister for British Schools. Valentine and Dinners took seats near the middle, once Dinners had set the children off writing their peer feedback about the Christmas launch.

They sat along the counter like cats eyeing each other. Front soon started laughing, nodding manically, broadcasting he was rising from the ashes, or in this case the sludge, of his latest adventure. Valentine and Dinners kept the volume low.

"What are you going to do now?"

"Isn't it obvious? Iphigenia's 'ere, me back at me school. Makin' me 'ead o' the school t' give t' other Val a rest. Ah insisted on doin' some teachin', though. Best job in t' world when yer allowed to do it prop'ly. Cosmina's joinin' me team. What about you?"

"I'm ready to become a human being again after long enough as a human doing. I was hoping to write my memoirs in a new political era, but he's still on top, the schooling revolution's still on, and he's going to be able to buy enough votes with his subsidised DIY to win the next election. And what about all the collateral damage? Not a great example, but what about Spads? At the end of the day, he just wants to make a contribution."

"Don't worry 'bout 'im. Cosmina signed 'im up f'r our dissolvin' products."

"If his shopping hits a wall, that'll be some case study!"

"Talkin' o' case studies ..." Dinners put a finger to his lips.

"Yes, government rev 1 news conference in the New Year ... You're right; we need radical change at Schools to get government rev 2 back on track. Clear out these awful special advisers completely. Get more teachers in there. If anyone can make these policies work, they can."

Dinners cracked a mischievous grin.

"See, Val? Iphigenia's already settin' up a proper schoolin' jackpot. They've never let a load o' teachers in t' Whitehall b'fore. It's the best chance we've 'ad yet t' make 'im fully accountable f'r summat."

www.ingramcontent.com/pod-product-compliance
Lightning Source LLC
Chambersburg PA
CBHW071013180726
48291CB00004B/1435